DISNEP

HIGH SCHOOL MUSICAL

STORIES FROM EAST HIGH #3

POETRY IN MOTION

By Alice Alfonsi

Based on the Disney Channel Original Movie
High School Musical, written by Peter Barsocchini

DISNEP
CHANNEL

PaRRagon

Bath New York Singapore Hong Kong Cologne Delhi Melbourne

Grateful acknowledgment is made to the following:

Lord Byron. "She Walks in Beauty", page 45.
Shakespeare, William. "Sonnet XVIII", pages 43–44.
Whitman, Walt. "I Hear America Singing", page 44.

This edition published by Parragon in 2008
Parragon
Queen Street House
4 Queen Street
Bath BA1 1HE, UK

ISBN 978-1-4075-3134-2

Printed in UK

CHAPTER ONE

Troy Bolton stifled a yawn. At the front of the room, Ms Barrington was reading yet another Scottish ode.

English was Troy's first class after lunch. Today he'd downed two cartons of milk and a turkey sandwich – good choices for athletic nutrition but a seriously bad combo for listening to two-hundred-year-old poetry. Pinching the back of his hand, Troy tried to stay alert. But his eyelids felt as if they'd been loaded down with free weights. His head dropped once, twice, three times. Then – *bop!* A little paper aeroplane hit him. Troy sat up straight. He was definitely awake now.

The tiny projectile had dropped onto his desk. He picked it up and unfolded the paper. Right away, he recognized the neat, delicate handwriting. . . .

O stay awake, Troy Bolton!
Push your comprehension.
'Cause if you nod off one more time,
You'll be napping in detention!

Poetically yours,
Gabriella

Before he could stop himself, Troy laughed out loud.

At the front of the room, the teacher looked up from her textbook. "Is something *funny*, Mr Bolton?"

"No, Ms Barrington," Troy said. He quickly

crumpled the note, hiding it in his fist.

The tall, slender teacher peered at him through her black oval-shaped glasses. Ms Barrington wasn't very old, but her floor-length skirts, severely upswept red hair and love of eighteenth-century poetry made her seem ancient to Troy.

"It certainly *sounds* as though you found something amusing in Robert Burns's poem," she said. "Why don't you share it with us?"

Troy silently groaned. Gabriella Montez was sitting in the next row. She'd been smiling at him when he read her funny note. Now that it had triggered trouble, she looked really upset.

Sorry, she silently mouthed to Troy.

It's okay, he mouthed back.

Ms Barrington tapped her foot. "Mr Bolton? I'm waiting." She glanced at Gabriella and narrowed her eyes. "Enlighten us. What exactly made you laugh?"

"Umm . . ." Troy swallowed. He felt heat rising in his cheeks.

Gabriella was about to speak up when a voice came from across the room.

"My man wasn't laughing," Chad Danforth insisted.

Ms Barrington put a hand on her hip and turned her head. Now she had a new target. "Is that right, Mr Danforth?"

Troy froze. Chad was one of his best friends. He always watched Troy's back, especially on the basketball court. But now was not the time for his team-mate to execute a fake-out!

"Straight up," Chad said. "You misheard Troy. He was just clearing his throat."

Ms Barrington narrowed her gaze. "I misheard him?"

"Sure," Chad said. "I mean, what dude in his right mind would laugh at what you just read?"

Troy cringed. "Uh, right. Sorry to interrupt, Ms Barrington. I just had to, you know, clear my dry throat. Like Chad said."

"You see how powerful that poem was?" Chad

went on. "Like subliminal advertising or some-thing."

"All right, Chad. That's enough." Ms Barrington cleared her own throat. "Let's move on, shall we?"

"Okay by me," Chad mumbled, exchanging a glance with his team-mates sitting in the back row. Two points, he silently mouthed to them.

Zeke Baylor and Jason Cross quietly sniggered and Troy exhaled with relief. He had no doubt that Chad had just saved him and Gabriella from all the joys of detention.

At the front of the room, Ms Barrington lifted her chin and addressed the class. "For the last four weeks, you've all been studying a number of poets. Now it's time to test what you've absorbed."

She snapped her textbook shut and leaned back against the edge of her desk. "But I'm not going to give you a traditional multiple-choice quiz. In my view, that's not the best way to test whether you've really learned what poetry is all about. Next Tuesday, at a special school assembly, each of you will read an original poem. This assignment will be a very important part of your semester grade. But I'm sure each of you will rise to the occasion."

Chad scratched his head of floppy brown hair. "Excuse me, Ms Barrington?" He waved his hand. "What do you mean, each of us will 'read an original poem'?"

The English teacher frowned. "What's not to understand, Chad? You will write a poem. Then you will read the poem you wrote. Simple."

"But . . ." Chad blinked. "In front of the whole school?"

"Yes, in front of the whole school. As I said, it's a very special assembly." Ms Barrington clapped her hands.

"So, will you accept poems written in any style?" Taylor McKessie asked, turning to a fresh page in her notebook. "Or just the Romantic style?" She lifted her pen, ready to scribble a detailed answer.

"Any style of poetry is welcome," Ms Barrington said. "We've covered a number of them in class and I've given you all a reading list. Inspiration abounds! Take advantage of it."

Kelsi Neilsen's hand went up. She nervously pushed up her round glasses. "Ms Barrington?" she asked, her small voice barely rising above the brim of her cap. "You're not really going to make it mandatory that we read our own poems, are you?"

"Of course!" Ms Barrington boomed. "Reading your own poetry is a vital experience and an essential part of the assignment."

Now Sharpay Evans raised her hand. "I, for one, think it's a brilliant assignment! Thank you, Ms Barrington, for giving us this opportunity to spotlight our individual talents!"

Ms Barrington nodded. "You're welcome, Sharpay."

Troy noticed Taylor rolling her eyes. Gabriella just sighed. Then the bell rang and everyone scattered.

* * *

"Dude, I owe you," Troy said, walking up to Chad a few minutes later. "Thanks for the save back there."

"No problem," Chad said. "Just pay me back with some sweet passes on the court."

"You got it," Troy smiled, and the two sealed the deal by knocking fists.

Taylor McKessie tossed Chad a warm smile as she walked into the hallway. "Easy assignment, huh, Chad?" she called.

"The assignment?" Chad said, automatically tensing. "Uh . . . sure . . . piece o' cake," he told her, forcing a smile and trying to seem relaxed.

The moment Taylor was gone, he grimaced. "As if I'm going to do it," he whispered to Troy. "Yeah, right."

Troy blinked. "What do you mean?"

"I'm not doing that poetry assignment," Chad said. "That's what I mean."

Troy couldn't believe what he was hearing.

"Chad, you have to. You heard Ms Barrington. It's a big part of your semester grade."

Chad waved his hand. "I'll tell her I've got writer's block or something. She'll let me off the hook. But I am *not* getting up on East's assembly hall stage, in front of the entire school, spouting rhymes about rainbows and red, red roses. This whole poetry thing freaks me out!"

"Freaks you out?" Sharpay piped up, over-hearing him. She tossed her blond hair and threw a special grin Troy's way. "What's the biggie, guys? Roses are red, violets are blue. The *writing* is simple. What's key is the *presentation*. Just find the right costume, practise in front of a mirror and you'll do fine!"

Chad looked horrified.

Sharpay didn't notice. She checked her watch. "Sorry, I've got to run," she chirped, dashing off. "Drama class next, and I haven't warmed my vocal cords! Buh-bye!"

Chad shuddered. He turned to Troy. "Did you hear what she said?" he whispered. "A *costume*?"

9

"Oh, wow. That's right. I forgot." Troy smacked his forehead, suddenly remembering. "Your leotard incident."

"Dude, don't even go there." Chad shook his head, looking a little sick to his stomach. He glanced around, making sure no one was close enough to hear.

Troy didn't blame him. When they were in the fourth grade, their teacher had convinced Chad to recite a poem at the Albuquerque Renaissance Fair. Unfortunately, she'd failed to warn him that he'd have to wear Elizabethan tights, silk bloomers and a hat with a feather.

All the boys in their class were laughing hysterically at him the second he stepped onto the stage. Chad had memorized the love poem perfectly. He was actually hoping to impress a girl named Rhonda. But when he saw every boy in his class laughing in the front row, he forgot the lines and began to stammer. Then he dropped his hat, bent over to pick it up, and his bloomers split open.

It wasn't a good day.

Six months later, Rhonda moved to Denver. But Chad never forgot the look on her face as he ran off the stage, mortified.

"I can't do it, man," Chad whispered. "I just can't."

"But—"

"Sorry." Chad shook his head. "I'll catch you later!"

Troy stood like a statue in the hallway. A couple of kids bumped into him. He didn't notice. He was too upset by what Chad intended to do –

Troy doubted that Ms Barrington was going to let anyone off the hook for this assignment. Their English teacher was really tough. She'd never accept an excuse of 'writer's block'.

Chad wasn't doing well in her class, either. And if she gave him a D or an F on his next report card, he'd get thrown off the basketball team for sure. That wasn't just school policy, it was Troy's dad's rule. All of Coach Bolton's players had to earn a C or higher in every class to stay on the team.

The Wildcats were everything to Chad. He'd be devastated if he couldn't play. And the team needed him. He was one of their best players!

A little frantically, he looked around for the one person he could confide in. Halfway down the hall he spied her – Gabriella Montez.

CHAPTER TWO

"**G**abriella!" Troy called. "We need to talk."

Gabriella was chatting with Taylor McKessie. Their Scholastic Decathlon team was going to sponsor a series of guest lectures. But the team members couldn't decide on a subject.

"Whoa," Taylor said, seeing Troy rushing up to them. "Something sounds urgent. What's up?"

"Nothing," Troy lied. "I just need to talk to Gabriella, *alone*."

Taylor shrugged. "Guess I'll see you in chemistry," she told Gabriella. Then she began to walk away.

As Troy waited for Taylor to move out of earshot, Gabriella touched his arm. "Listen, Troy, I'm really sorry about the note," she began. "I didn't mean to—"

"Your note was hilarious," he assured her. "And it kept me from being caught sleeping. This isn't about your note." He lowered his voice. "It's about Chad."

"Chad?" said Gabriella.

She looked confused. To Troy, she also looked really pretty in her silky ice blue blouse and white ruffled skirt. A tiny blue hair slide sparkled in her long dark hair, and for a second he felt mesmerized.

Sometimes being close to Gabriella made Troy forget everything else. He wished they could just talk about seeing a movie on the weekend or grabbing a smoothie after school. But this was too important to put on hold. Blinking his eyes,

Troy forced himself to focus. After swearing her to secrecy, he quietly explained Chad's problem.

"I see," Gabriella said when he finally fell silent. "So because of what happened to Chad in the fourth grade, he hates poetry?"

"Chad doesn't hate poetry. And he doesn't have stage fright, either. He likes being the center of attention. Chad is . . . I don't know . . ." Troy's voice trailed off.

"Poetically challenged?" Gabriella suggested.

"It's more panic than anything else," Troy said.

Gabriella nodded, tapping her chin. "So he's got poetry phobia?"

Troy smiled. "Yeah, sure, Doctor," he told Gabriella. "Since that's your diagnosis, have you got a cure for the dude?"

"Cure?"

"You know, like, 'Take two nursery rhymes and call me in the morning'?"

Gabriella laughed. "I think there's only one solution: you have to talk to him again. You're his best friend. He'll listen to you."

"I just *tried* to talk to him."

"Well, try again," Gabriella urged. "You heard Ms Barrington. It's an important part of his grade."

Just then, the warning bell rang. They were both going to be late for their next class if they didn't get going.

"Let's talk after school," Gabriella told Troy. "I'll meet you by your locker before basketball practice. Okay?"

Troy nodded. "Okay."

But it wasn't okay. And by the end of the next period, the situation had got worse. Chad's nervousness about the assignment spread like a fever to Zeke Baylor and Jason Cross. Now more than half of the Wildcats' first-string basketball team was freaked about the assignment.

Troy decided to talk to their teacher. If he just explained how upset the guys were, maybe Ms Barrington would reconsider the whole writing-and-reciting thing. Maybe she'd decide to give the class a typical multiple-choice test instead.

During his free period, Troy returned to Ms Barrington's classroom. But the English teacher wasn't there. He asked around and found her in the assembly hall, standing on the stage with the drama teacher, Ms Darbus.

"I think a plain black backdrop will be fine," Ms Barrington said to Ms Darbus.

Ms Darbus nodded. "If we close the down-stage curtain, it will cover the standing set. Then the drama club won't have to move a thing. And you can create a nice mood with the footlights."

"Can we have a spotlight, too?" Ms Barrington asked.

"Of course!" Ms Darbus snapped her fingers. "What is a dramatic poetry reading without a spotlight!"

Both women laughed.

Troy suddenly felt a little nervous approaching Ms Barrington. But then he thought of how Chad had helped him out earlier in class and he stepped up.

"Ms Barrington?" Troy called. "Can I talk to you?"

"May I," she said, peering down at him through her black, oval glasses.

"May you what?" Troy asked.

Ms Barrington sighed. "Troy, the correct way to phrase your question is 'May I?' not 'Can I?'"

"Oh, right. Got it. So . . . *may I*?"

Ms Barrington nodded. "Yes. Speak."

Troy noticed a few kids from the drama club hanging close by. He didn't want to broadcast this conversation, so he asked the teacher, "Can we . . . I mean, *may* we speak in private, please?"

Ms Barrington nodded and led him into the wings. A red velvet curtain hung down, partially blocking them from view.

"I'm really sorry to bother you," Troy began. "But this is important." He spent the next few minutes trying to explain how nervous Chad was about next week's poetry reading assembly. Troy tried to persuade her to change the event to a regular test.

But Ms Barrington remained unconvinced. "Chad's one of the most outgoing students I have," she said. "He won't have any trouble reciting a poem. Don't you remember how much fun he had onstage during East High's first annual Battle of the Bands?"

"But to Chad, this is different," Troy argued, "a lot different. In fact, I think he's so nervous he might even have writer's block."

Ms Barrington folded her arms. "I'm not going to let anyone off the hook for this assignment, Troy. As I told you in class, this is going to be an important part of the semester grade, and I expect everyone to complete it."

"But other kids are nervous, too," Troy pointed out, thinking of Kelsi Neilsen as well as Zeke and Jason. "Some of your students are shy. They're not comfortable with standing in front of an audience, let alone reading their own poetry."

"Oh, Troy!" Ms Barrington shook her head. "That's why this assignment is so important for them to complete. They must learn how to rise to the occasion."

"But–"

"Remember when you helped Gabriella during your audition for the school's *Twinkle Towne* musical?" asked the teacher. "I saw how nervous she was. But you helped her overcome her fears. And both of you performed beautifully! So if you're that worried about your friends, then you should help them, like you helped Gabriella. And if–"

Just then, the drama teacher called out from the back of the assembly hall. "Ms Barrington! Where are you? I'd like you to observe the lighting scheme!"

Ms Barrington stepped past the red velvet curtain. "I'll be there in just a moment!" she called from the wings. Then she turned back to Troy.

"You know what?" she said. "I'm going to tell you a secret. Next week's special assembly is really in honour of an old college friend of mine.

He's an award-winning poet, and I've promised to show him how brightly my students shine when it comes to writing and reciting poetry. Julius is going to judge the poems. He'll be picking the runners-up and the winner."

"Winner?" Troy asked. "Winner of what?"

Ms Barrington grinned. "The winning poem will be published in the local paper, along with the winning student's photo. I was going to keep it a surprise. But I think you ought to tell your classmates. It's just one more reason any student who doesn't do this assignment will be given a failing grade. I intend to see *every* member of my class recite in front of Julius!"

Troy tried to think of another argument, but he couldn't. And a moment later, the teacher was gone.

"Arrrgh!" Troy cried in frustration before striding away.

* * *

"Did you hear that?" Sharpay Evans hissed from behind the curtain.

Her brother, Ryan, scratched his head. "*Arrrgh?*"

"No, lamebrain!" Sharpay snapped.

Ryan had been helping his sister in the wings. She'd been pawing through a trunk of costumes, looking for the perfect outfit to wear at next week's assembly. That's when they'd overheard the English teacher talking to Troy. Now Sharpay knew the big secret.

"Next week's assembly is really a poetry contest. The winner will be published in the newspaper! Do you know what that means?" she asked her brother.

Ryan scratched his head again. "There'll be less room for classified ads?"

Sharpay swatted her brother. "I'm going be famous!"

"Because . . . ?" Ryan still didn't get it.

"I'm going to come up with the winning poem. I'll get my name and picture in the paper. My poem will actually be *published*. Then all of my classmates will be totally jealous. Fame is so sweet, I can almost taste it!"

"Oh, *puh-lease*," a voice muttered on the other side of the curtain.

Sharpay frowned. Now it sounded like someone was eavesdropping on *her*. "Who's there?" she demanded, pulling aside the curtain.

"It's me," said Taylor McKessie.

"You've got a lot of nerve listening to other people's conversations!" Sharpay cried.

Ryan's brow wrinkled. "But weren't you and I just—"

Sharpay's fists clenched. "Shut up, Ryan!"

"Sorry," Taylor said. "I didn't mean to eavesdrop. I was looking for Ms Barrington, and someone told me she stepped into the wings."

"Well, she's not here now," said Sharpay. "You missed her again. But I've got a news flash for you. If you're trying to butter her up to win that poetry contest, don't bother. I'm the one who's going to have her poem and picture published in the newspaper."

23

Taylor rolled her eyes. "I was looking for Ms Barrington so I could return a book I borrowed from her." She held up the collection of Shakespeare's sonnets. "But you know what, Sharpay? If you're right and this assignment is also going to be a contest to get a poem published, you're deluding yourself if you think you're going to win."

"Is that right?" Sharpay folded her arms.

"Yes. If the assignment were *Dancing with the Stars*, you'd have an advantage," Taylor said, pointing to Sharpay's long legs. "But writing good poetry takes a high I.Q. so you don't stand a chance of winning."

"And who does, Einstein-ette?" Sharpay asked. "You?"

Taylor shrugged. "I haven't really thought about it."

"Do you really think you can beat me at this?" Sharpay challenged.

Taylor sighed. Going head-to-head with Sharpay on a school assignment was really beneath her. But the more Taylor considered it, the more she liked the idea of seeing her own poem in the paper. After all, the words "published poet" would look awfully good on those future Ivy League college applications.

"You know what?" Taylor said.

"What?" Sharpay snapped.

Hands on hips, Taylor stepped forward till the girls were nose-to-nose. "Bring it on."

CHAPTER THREE

"I'm really looking forward to practice today," Troy told Gabriella after school. They were walking side-by-side toward the gymnasium. "A couple of hundred layup shots *might* make me feel better."

Since he'd failed to persuade Ms Barrington to change the assignment, he had to think of another way to help his friends.

He was about to ask Gabriella for advice when she tapped him on the shoulder. "Troy," she whispered, pointing down the hallway. "Look."

Outside the gym doors, Chad, Zeke and Jason were huddled together in a circle of misery. Chad was frowning. Zeke was groaning. And Jason was shaking his head.

"They must be talking about the poetry assignment," Troy whispered to Gabriella. "This is my first chance to talk to them all together. Come with me, okay?"

"Sure," she told him.

Troy walked up to his team-mates. "What's up, guys?"

Jason frowned. "You know what's up."

Chad nodded. "That stupid assignment for Ms Barrington's class."

"I can whip up a batch of flaky croissants or a perfect soufflé like that," said Zeke, snapping his fingers. "But putting words together? Man, that's just not my thing."

"And did you hear the afternoon announcements?" Jason said. "Barrington's making this whole thing a contest, which means our poems are going to be judged in front of the entire school!"

Chad turned to Troy. "I was telling them my idea. We could all say we have writer's block. What do you think?"

"Group writer's block?" Troy said. "It's not going to work, and I'll tell you why. I already talked to Ms Barrington."

Troy told the guys how he'd gone to bat for them. "She refuses to accept any excuse. We all have to do this assignment, or we're cooked. We'll end up with rotten semester grades. And then—"

"We'll be off the team," Chad said. He shook his head and sighed. "Man, I hate to say it. But you're right. Getting kicked off the team would be worse than anything."

"Listen, none of you has to fail," Troy insisted. "You just need to get your head in the zone. You can do it. All of you can."

The guys stared at him.

"Really?" Chad said. "How?"

Troy froze. He hadn't figured out the next step yet. But he was the team captain and the guys were looking at him, counting on him. Desperate, he turned to the girl standing behind him.

"Gabriella's great at poetry," he declared. "She'll help you!"

Gabriella's eyes widened. "Me?"

Troy saw her deer-in-the-headlights look and dragged her into the huddle. "Come on. You don't want to see these dudes fail, do you?"

Gabriella shook her head. "No, of course not."

"Well," said Troy, "all you have to do is teach them how to write a really good poem."

Gabriella pulled Troy aside. "I don't know if I can do that," she whispered.

"Sure you can," Troy replied. "You're an A grade student. You get top marks in everything, including English. If anyone can help these guys, you can."

Gabriella looked up. Four pairs of desperate eyes were staring at her. *Whoa*, she thought. Talk about pressure!

"Are you going to help us?" Zeke asked.

Gabriella swallowed uneasily. She couldn't let them down. "Let's meet at Bob's Burgers after practice," she told them. "Then we can get started."

"Bob's Burgers?" Jason said in horror. "Are you crazy?"

"No way," Zeke agreed.

"You're not helping us write poetry in *public*," Chad hissed.

"Okay, okay," Gabriella said with a sigh. "How about my house, then? Eight o'clock? Is that private enough for you?"

"Sun's down by eight, right?" Chad whispered to his friends.

Zeke and Jason nodded.

"Okay," he said. "We're there."

The early-evening desert sky was purple and sprinkled with stars. But away from the glow of the streetlight, Troy, Chad, Zeke and Jason moved in shadow.

"All clear?" Chad asked. Beneath a dark blue hood, his eyes scanned the seemingly empty suburban street.

Jason peered from behind a bush. "Clear."

"All clear," agreed Zeke, emerging from behind a tree.

Troy sighed as he stepped around a parked car. "Chad, don't you think you're overreacting? I didn't see anyone from the school paper on our trail."

"Oh, no," Chad warned. "You never actually *see* them. You just see a totally embarrassing picture of yourself on the front page of the school paper the next day."

"But what we're doing is no big deal," Troy insisted.

"Dude," Chad said, "consider the photo caption. 'After their hard-driving practice, East's starting players get together for an evening of writing poetry at Gabriella Montez's house.'"

Troy frowned. "I see what you mean."

"It would be even worse than the last time I

got my picture in the paper," Chad pointed out.

"You mean when you lost that pizza-eating contest to a sixth-grade girl?" Jason asked.

Chad groaned. "I really didn't need to have that documented in print. Not with sauce all over my face and pepperoni stuck in my hair."

"And that little girl holding the pizza trophy over your head." Zeke laughed. "But you have to admit, the pepperoni in your hair was funny."

Chad shook his head. "I'll never eat pizza again."

"Okay, you win," said Troy. "Let's move, but keep low."

The team raced across the lawn to the front porch. Troy knocked quietly. When no one answered, he knocked again, just a little louder.

Finally the door opened. Gabriella's mother saw them and smiled. "I thought someone knocked. But you were so quiet, I hardly heard you!" she loudly declared. "Are you all here for your poetry lesson?"

"Shhhh!" the boys hissed in unison.

"Sorry," Ms Montez said, lowering her voice. "Come on in."

Gabriella greeted them and led the boys to the living room. She'd borrowed her mum's kitchen blackboard and had written a few – okay, *a lot* of – notes about different types of poetry and rhyming styles.

Gabriella didn't know how much the notes would help. Mostly she hoped the classroom atmosphere would help the boys focus. Instead, they groaned when they saw the blackboard.

Not a good start, Gabriella thought. And she began to wonder if she really could help them. If this were maths or science, she could teach them hard facts, no problem. But poetry was like music. You could teach someone notes on a musical scale, but playing well was more than putting notes together. You had to have a feel for it. While everyone had feelings, no two people were alike emotionally.

"Okay, let's forget the blackboard," Gabriella

said as the boys settled on the sofa. She heard their relieved sighs.

"Basically, poetry is a picture you paint with words," she began. "So let's start by visualizing a picture. Close your eyes and imagine you're in a colourful garden full of flowers and trees. . . "

Troy closed his eyes and leaned back. Chad did the same. Reluctantly, Jason and Zeke also closed their eyes.

"Okay," Gabriella continued. "Do you have a picture of a garden in your mind?"

The boys nodded.

"Good. Now start describing the amazing things you see." Gabriella expected to hear about pastel flower petals and dappled sunlight.

Eyes still closed, Chad spoke first. "Bugs," he announced. "I see bugs!"

"Yeah!" Zeke cried. "Really gross ones with eighteen legs."

"And snakes!" said Chad. "Really cool snakes, like copperheads and rattlers!"

"Awesome," said Troy. "I see a slimy slug.

He's puffy and round and pink. And he's leaving a slime trail across a flower that looks kind of silver in the sun."

"Deep," said Jason. "You know, I once saw a praying mantis eat an ant. Do you think that image would make for a good poem?"

Gabriella shuddered. The boys were choosing fairly disgusting images. But hey, she thought, these are their poems, not mine!

"Okay," she said gamely. "Open your eyes. Now each of you write a poem that reflects the picture you saw in your mind."

She passed out paper and pencils, and soon the boys were scribbling. Gabriella waited ten minutes. Then she asked them to read what they wrote.

Troy went first. "The slug crawled across a flower of orange and left a trail of silver."

"Go on," said Gabriella.

"That's as far as I got," Troy replied. "I couldn't think of any words that rhymed with 'orange' or 'silver.'"

Gabriella frowned. Troy had actually picked

the only two words in the English language that didn't have rhymes.

What were the odds?

She tried to stay positive. "It's okay, Troy. You know, poems don't have to rhyme."

Shifting her gaze to Jason, she asked him to read.

He nodded and began. "The praying mantis was munching away./He made the ant his meal today./The poor little ant gave all he got./Under his shell, his guts looked like snot—"

"That's enough," Gabriella cried. She shuddered, then cleared her throat. "What did you write, Zeke?"

"Little bug with eighteen legs./If they got cut off, you'd be walking on pegs—"

Oh, wow, Gabriella thought. They're just getting worse.

"Chad — you're next," she said, gritting her teeth.

But Chad just shook his head. "I tried to write a poem about snakes. Copperheads, rattlers, maybe even a boa constrictor. Then I got to thinking about that constrictor play North Central tried on us a few weeks back—"

"That was a killer," Zeke agreed. "They had me so boxed in I couldn't move, couldn't even pass the ball—"

Jason moaned. "They had my head so messed up I got whistled three times for travelling."

"Guys!" Gabriella cried in frustration. "No basketball!"

Chad rolled his eyes. "Come on, Teach," he teased. "Loosen up."

Troy stood up. "I'm totally backing Gabriella on this," he said. "Right now, it's poetry time. Not basketball time."

Chad shook his head. "We *know* basketball. That's easy to talk about. Poetry is still a mystery."

"Well, if you want to keep playing basketball, it's a mystery you'd better solve," Troy replied. "So let's get our heads *out* of the game – and *into* the poetry. I've already started my poem for Ms Barrington."

"You have? What are you writing?" Zeke asked.

Troy shrugged. "It's right here in my notebook."

"But what is it? What's it about?" Jason asked.

"Yeah, I'd like to know," said Chad.

Gabriella spoke up. "I'd like to know, too. It might help us all."

But Troy looked away. He actually blushed a little. "It's not done yet," he told them. "Until I finish it, I don't want to say what it's about."

Suddenly, it hit Gabriella. The way Troy was blushing, she was sure he'd written a poem about her – about them. Now she understood. He was too embarrassed to admit it in front of his friends. She could understand why he felt that way, but she couldn't wait to hear it!

"Okay," Gabriella said. "Maybe we should try the visual exercise again–"

A loud knock at the door suddenly interrupted her.

"Hide!" Chad cried. "It's the press!"

CHAPTER FOUR

"**H**ey, there," said Taylor McKessie, who was standing there when Gabriella opened the door.

"You didn't see anyone from the school paper, did you?" Gabriella asked, curiously peering over her friend's shoulder.

"Just little old me." Taylor shrugged. "So, Professor, how's the poetry lesson coming?"

Gabriella moaned. "So far it's Disaster 101."

"I'm not surprised," Taylor said, folding her arms. "We're not just talking boys here. We're talking basketball players. I'll bet they're driving you buggy."

"I couldn't have put it better," Gabriella said, thinking about their insect-fest. "I'll never look at a garden the same way again."

"So, you sounded a little desperate on the phone earlier. Do you still want my help?" Taylor asked.

Gabriella nodded. "I can't get through to them. I hope you have a plan."

"You've got to be kidding." Taylor whipped a purple notebook out of her backpack. "When you're Chemistry Club president and captain of the Scholastic Decathlon Team, you *always* have a plan."

Gabriella walked Taylor into the living room.

When Chad Danforth saw her, he covered the paper he'd been scribbling on. "Hey, Taylor," he called. "We just came over for a little help with our biology homework–"

Taylor nodded and pulled the page out from under his hand. "Snake, snake, are you real or a trick?" she read. "Are your fangs poisonous or made of plastic?" She winced.

"It's *rhyming* biology homework, okay," Chad declared defensively.

Taylor lifted the blackboard and read the notes Gabriella had written on it. "Iambic pentameter?"

"Yeah, and that's iambic homework," Jason said lamely. "For my . . . um . . . iambic class."

Taylor rolled her eyes. "And I suppose you built a pentameter in woodwork class?"

Jason opened his mouth to speak, but Taylor raised a finger to silence him. "You guys don't have to lie to me. Gabriella told me about your issues, and I came over to help you learn the true essence of poetry."

"Which is?" Chad asked.

Taylor grinned. "Mathematics! Poetry is all about mathematics."

"It only gets worse," Jason said miserably.

Taylor set up the blackboard so everyone could see it. The boys groaned, but Taylor ignored them and pressed on. "Like music, which is also mathematical, most forms of poetry have a rhythm–"

"Yeah, but can you dance to it?" Chad cracked. Jason sniggered and Zeke slammed him a high five.

"The rhythm of poetry is made up of beats. And you measure beats in feet," Taylor explained.

"Big feet?" Jason joked. "Or little feet?"

"What size shoe do these feet wear?" Chad teased.

Taylor rolled her eyes. "Not those kinds of feet. Now be serious, guys! A foot is also called an iamb. Put five feet together and you have iambic pentameter–"

Jason put his hands over his ears and moaned. "My head is going to explode."

"I think we need an example," Zeke said.

"Sure," Taylor said. "It's like da-DUM is one foot or iamb. So da-DUM, da-DUM, da-DUM, da-DUM, da-DUM is a single line of iambic pentameter. One da-DUM repeated five times, see?"

"All right!" Zeke cried.

Troy nodded enthusiastically. "You understand it now, Zeke?"

"Actually, no," he replied.

"I don't either," said Jason.

"Yeah, Taylor, I guess right now, we're all feeling pretty da-DUMB," said Chad.

Gabriella and Taylor exchanged unhappy glances.

"I have an idea," Chad said. "Taylor, why don't you read us a poem *you* think is good."

"Sure, Chad. That's actually a great idea." Taylor pulled the purple notebook from the sleeve of her pack.

"This is my special poetry notebook," she explained, leafing through it. She searched until she found an example of iambic pentameter. Taylor cleared her throat and began to read:

"Shall I compare thee to a summer's day?
Thou art more lovely and more temperate:

Rough winds do shake the darling buds of May,
And summer's lease has all too short a date . . ."

"Whoa . . . that's really good," Chad said, clearly impressed. "Read another . . ."

"Here's one of my favorites," Taylor said. "It's not in iambic pentameter. It's in free verse. That basically means the meter and rhyme patterns aren't fixed."

Taylor then read "On the Pulse of Morning," by Maya Angelou. She read more poems, too – by Robert Frost, Billy Collins, and Nikki Giovanni.

"And here's another example of free verse," she said.

"I hear America singing, the varied carols I hear;
Those of mechanics – each one singing his, as it
*   should be, blithe and strong;*
The carpenter singing his, as he measures his
*   plank or beam,*
The mason singing his, as he makes ready for
*   work. . . ."*

"I could never write something like that," said Chad.

"Sure you could," Taylor replied, gazing at Chad. "You know, when you guys are off the court, you actually look somewhat civilized. Put your minds to it, and I'll bet you could write something like this." She turned the pages in her notebook again. "This one's called 'She Walks in Beauty.'"

Troy's ears perked up when he heard the title. He moved to the edge of his seat as Taylor began to read. . . .

"She walks in beauty, like the night
Of cloudless climes and starry skies,
And all that's best of dark and bright
Meet in her aspect and her eyes. . . ."

As Taylor read, Gabriella felt funny, like someone was watching her. She looked across the room and found Troy gazing right at her. When their eyes met, he smiled. Gabriella's heart raced. She blushed and looked away as Taylor continued reading. When she finished the poem, Taylor lowered her dog-eared purple notebook. There was a long moment of silence. Finally, Jason spoke.

"Whoa," he said.

Gabriella dared to look up again. Troy was still smiling at her! Does Troy really feel that way about me? she wondered. She shivered. It seemed amazing . . . impossible, and wonderful, too!

"Taylor, those were all awesome poems," Chad said. "Which one are you going to read next week?"

Taylor laughed. "No, no. I'm not reading any of those. I didn't write them. They were written by William Shakespeare, Walt Whitman and Lord Byron. I'm working on my own poem. Something new."

"Could you read us some of that poem?" Zeke asked.

"Well, I don't know. . . ." Then Taylor glanced

at her watch. "Oh!" she cried. "I didn't realize it was so late. I'm sorry, but I really have to go."

"No way," Chad protested.

"I'm really sorry, guys," Taylor insisted, tucking the purple notebook into its sleeve and donning her backpack.

Chad rose to help Taylor with her stuff. "Where are you going in such a hurry?" he asked.

"I'm supposed to meet Martha Cox at the observatory. We signed up for an astronomy lecture," Taylor explained. "If we like it, we'll invite the speaker to East High as the Scholastic Decathlon team's first guest lecturer."

"Taylor, wait," Chad called. "Before you go, could you tell us the secret of writing such awesome poetry?"

Taylor scanned the expectant faces in the room and scratched her head. Then she pulled out her notebook one more time.

"I was reading this book the other day. It's filled with letters from a famous poet to a younger poet who had asked for advice."

"What did he say?" Troy asked.

Taylor scanned her notes. "When you first start writing, keep it simple," she advised. "Just start writing about things in your everyday life." Taylor shrugged and looked up from her notebook. "Poetry is a way to see the world. Just open your eyes and look for inspiration all around you!"

Chad blinked. "And that's it?"

Taylor shrugged. "That's it. See you at school tomorrow. Good luck!"

Gabriella escorted Taylor to the front door. "Thanks, Taylor." She smiled. "I loved all the poems that you read."

"Yeah," said Taylor. "But I could see Troy really liked *one* more than any other. He was looking right at you when I read 'She Walks in Beauty.'"

Gabriella blushed. "He just liked the poem."

"Yeah, right!" Taylor laughed.

Gabriella smiled. "Well, the boys are inspired now. That's the main thing. Look at them over there, all talking a mile a minute. I think they're really excited to get started writing. That's the most important thing."

Taylor checked her watch again. "Yikes! Got to go. Martha and the solar system await!"

Gabriella said goodbye to her friend. When she returned to the living room, she found the guys getting ready to leave, too.

"Thanks for helping us," Chad said, heading for the front door. "I think maybe I can write a poem now. I'm still not sure I want to read it in front of the entire school, though."

"You'll do fine," Gabriella insisted.

"See you tomorrow," Zeke said, following Chad out. "And thanks for your help!"

"Taylor deserves all the thanks," Gabriella said modestly.

"Naw, you do, too," Jason called, heading out with his buds. "You're the man . . . er, I mean, the best!"

Troy hung back, pretending to fumble with his jacket. Finally, the other guys were gone and he and Gabriella were alone.

"I really appreciate what you did," Troy began. "For the guys. And me, too. I've never had a better lesson in poetry. . . ."

His voice trailed off as their eyes met.

"You're amazing, Gabriella," Troy gushed.

She grinned and lowered her eyes. "I can't wait to hear your poem, Troy," she whispered. "The one you said you already started."

Troy nodded. "I'm writing about something that's really special to me."

Gabriella felt a little dizzy.

"Well," Troy said, shifting nervously. "Guess I'd better go."

They walked to the front door together. "I'll see you tomorrow," Troy said softly, his gaze lingering on hers.

"Good night," Gabriella replied.

To her delight, Troy couldn't seem to tear his eyes away from her, even as he moved across the porch. He actually tripped and caught himself before he finally turned his head around and headed into the night.

CHAPTER FIVE

Gabriella closed the front door and floated back into her house. After taking the blackboard into the kitchen, she returned to the living room and straightened the couch cushions. That's when she noticed Troy's notebook.

"Oh, no," she whispered. "Troy left his notebook behind."

By now, Troy was long gone. She'd never catch up with him. But she knew it was no big deal. She would just take it with her to school

51

tomorrow and give it back to him then.

After turning off the living room lamps, Gabriella headed up to her bedroom. She was exhausted from the stress of the lesson, but she wanted to do some work on her own poem. It was about Troy, of course!

She'd scribbled a few lines in study period already. Now she read them over at her desk, wrote a few more lines, then found her mind wandering.

She reached for a book of poetry, hoping to find inspiration, and her hand bumped Troy's notebook. As it dropped to the bedroom floor, a few loose papers fell out.

It was clear from the writing on these papers that Troy had already started working on his poem, just like he'd said. Lines and words had been written, then crossed out and replaced with others. It was obvious that he'd spent a lot of time on it. Gabriella's gaze fell over the words as she picked up the papers. One clean stanza stood out immediately.

When we're together, my pulse races.
And I love to visit our favourite places.
Higher and higher, we soar as one.
Nothing on earth will stop our fun. . . .

Gabriella smiled. It wasn't Shakespeare or anything, but it was very sweet. Then her gaze moved to the title of the poem and her heart turned cold.

Ariel by Troy Bolton

Gabriella stared at the page in disbelief. But there was no denying it. The dark grey pencil was bold and sure. She looked at another piece of paper and saw more of the poem. It made her discovery even clearer.

When I'm down or lonely,
I roll with you and smile.
You take me to the limit.
You lift me, Ariel-style!

"He's not writing about me at all," she whispered. "He's crushing on some other girl . . . someone named Ariel."

Gabriella didn't know anyone by that name. Did she go to another school? Maybe she was an older girl or a friend of the Bolton family. Whoever she was, she'd obviously captured Troy's heart.

Shaking her head, Gabriella thought back to the moment Taylor had read that romantic poem, "She Walks in Beauty."

"I'm so stupid . . ." Gabriella whispered. "Troy wasn't thinking about me while Taylor was reciting that poem. He was thinking about Ariel."

Totally shattered, she placed the loose papers back in Troy's notebook and closed the cover.

Meanwhile, across town, Sharpay was working on her own poetry presentation.

"Whoa," Ryan said, walking into her room.

Skirts, pants, sparkle tops and dresses covered the bed. Scarves and handbags hung on every drawer handle. And shoes and hats covered the floor.

"Did a twister just blow through here?" Ryan asked his sister. "Or are you hoping to strike gold lamé at the bottom of your wardrobe?"

"Very funny," Sharpay snapped. She wheeled, marched out of her wardrobe, and strode across the room. "I still need to find the perfect poetry-reading outfit."

Ryan frowned. "You didn't like *any* of those costumes in the drama club trunk?"

"No. They were all too obviously theatrical." She began to pace. "I need something that speaks more authentically to my role."

"I see," Ryan said. "So what are you going for?"

"That's the trouble. I have too many choices. Look . . ." She rushed to the bed and picked up a psychedelic minidress. "I could do Flamboyant Performance Artist."

"Fab," said Ryan.

"Or . . ." She threw down the psychedelic

dress and picked up a grey flannel business suit. "I could do Serious Professional Writer."

"Ugh," said Ryan. "Looks more like Serious Professional Bank Examiner."

"Okay, how about . . ." She threw down the suit, shoved on a dark beret and held up a black turtleneck and stretch pants.

"What's that?" Ryan asked.

"Angst-Ridden Poetess." Sharpay showed Ryan her profile and displayed a grim expression.

"Hmmmm," said Ryan, considering the three choices. "While number three says 'I have deep thoughts', number two says 'show me the money' and number one says 'pair me with go-go boots'."

"This isn't the Battle of the Bands, Ryan! This is a public poetry reading. Ms Barrington's friend is an award-winning writer. That means this Julius person has got to be very serious and deep. I think I should go with outfit number three."

"It's your call then, I guess." Ryan walked over to Sharpay's desk. "Maybe if I read your poem, I could give you better advice on the outfit."

"No! No! That's okay!" Sharpay tried to stop her brother. But it was too late. He'd already seen what was written on her laptop screen.

Ryan cleared his throat and began to read:

"Shoes, shoes, how I love them.
Let me count the styles.
Mules, boots, slippers, slingbacks,
leathers and crocodiles . . ."

Ryan paused. "Wow, Sharpay," he murmured. "This is tragically bad." He pushed the scroll-down button to read more, but the rest of the screen was blank. "And you've only written one stanza."

"I know." Sharpay pushed aside a pile of clothes and flopped onto her bed.

"Well, don't you think you should maybe

spend more time writing the poem than picking out clothes for the day you recite it?"

Sharpay sighed. "The truth is . . . scribbling is not my strength. I'm really better at staging and recitation than actually writing this stuff. But I can't let Taylor McKessie get the best of me. I can't!"

"I agree." Ryan nodded. "And you know what they say in the theatre. The show must go on!"

Sharpay blinked. "What does that have to do with writing poetry?"

"Nothing, really." Ryan shrugged. "I just find that saying to be very inspiring."

Sharpay rolled her eyes. "You should be telling me to keep at it. You know, 'If at first you don't succeed . . .'"

"Oh, right! Try, try again! I know that one." He paused, cleared his throat, and in a serious voice declared: "If at first you don't succeed, try, try—"

"Stop! I get it!" Sharpay rose and walked to her laptop. She reread the four lines she'd written. "Anyway, that's easy for you to say. You don't have to write an award-winning poem."

"You're right. I don't," he said, turning to go. " 'Cause I'm not in your English class."

"Ryan?" Sharpay called as her brother headed for the door.

"Yes?" he replied.

"You wouldn't . . ." she began in a sheepish voice. "You wouldn't have any suggestions, would you?"

Ryan stopped at the door and faced his sister. "Well, I'm no literary expert or anything, but maybe your shoes aren't the best subject for a poem."

"They're not?" Sharpay said. "Then what should I write about instead?"

Ryan glanced around the room and chewed his lip in thought. "Your handbags?"

CHAPTER SIX

Troy couldn't stop thinking about all the amazing things Gabriella and Taylor had said about poetry. That night, before he went to bed, he decided the poem he'd begun to write about Ariel wasn't good enough. He was going to compose a brand-new poem.

Starting tomorrow morning, I'm going to view the world through the eyes of a poet, he told himself. I'll look for poetic inspiration in all the ordinary, everyday things in my life. . .

60

At breakfast the next day, instead of gulping down his food, Troy decided to contemplate his waffles. He tried to find inspiration in the way the butter and syrup formed little lakes of flavour in each square. He rummaged through the dictionary for words to describe the way his nose savoured the smell of warm maple and sugary dough.

Unfortunately, Troy searched for inspiration for so long that the waffles got cold. He had to warm them up in the microwave.

On his way to school, Troy noticed the clouds. Eyes to the sky, he tried to express the fluffy, ever-changing shapes in words. He didn't have much luck – and he also walked into a stop sign.

After he arrived at school, Troy lingered at his locker. He watched his classmates, listened to their voices and considered how to describe all the sounds they made in the corridors – the shuffling, banging and shouting.

He stood marvelling at the way the noise grew

louder and louder until the late bell rang. Then it quickly dropped into a whispering silence as the swarms of students melted away, drifting through classroom doors.

That's when Troy realized he was standing in the middle of an empty hallway. And the late bell had rung already.

Dashing off to his tutor room, he barely made registration. Ms Darbus didn't appreciate his artistic excuse. She gave him fifteen minutes of detention for being tardy.

Man, Troy thought. How do real poets get anything done?

After first period, Sharpay was refreshing her make-up in her locker mirror when Ryan rushed up to her.

"Sharpay! Sharpay!" he cried.

"Darn it, Ryan! You made me smudge my lip liner!"

"Forget your lip liner!" He lowered his voice. "I heard some juicy gossip."

Sharpay's eyes widened. She recapped her liner pen and faced her brother. "Spill!"

"I heard a rumour during my last class," he said. "Apparently, Taylor McKessie has already written a bunch of poems."

"Did you say *poems*?" Sharpay's face fell. "As in plural? More than one?"

"And all of her poems are amazing!" Ryan exclaimed. "She read them out of her purple notebook at Gabriella's house last night. Some of the guys on the basketball team were talking about them. It sounds like they were really impressed with what she read."

Sharpay seethed. She couldn't believe Taylor was going to beat her so easily.

"Sounds like Taylor's really bringing it," Ryan told his sister.

"It does, doesn't it?"

"So what are you going to do?"

Sharpay slammed her locker door shut. "Bring it right back, of course!"

"How?"

"Drastic times call for drastic measures."

"What does that mean, exactly?" Ryan asked.

"Come with me and I'll show you."

"Ms Barrington?" Sharpay knocked lightly on her English teacher's classroom's door.

"Yes?" Ms Barrington looked up from the pile of homework she'd been marking.

"Ms Barrington, I was wondering something about next week's assignment."

"Yes?" asked the teacher.

"Would you, by any chance, be open to a poem that's written by more than one student?"

Ms Barrington's eyebrows rose. She was silent for a long moment. Sharpay tensed, waiting for her reaction. Finally, the teacher's face broke into a grin.

"What a splendid idea, Sharpay!" she cried. "I must say, I'm impressed."

"You are?" Sharpay was stunned. She thought her chances of convincing the teacher were slim to none.

"Collaboration is an exciting way to write a poem," said Ms Barrington. "There are stellar examples in literature of two or more authors working on the same poem. And any of my students ambitious enough to explore this method are more than welcome to try it. Good luck!"

"Thanks," said Sharpay.

Rushing out of the classroom, she felt a little light-headed. She'd not only got approval, she'd got praise from the teacher for proposing it!

"That's great," said Ryan, who'd been eavesdropping in the doorway. "But who are you going to get to collaborate with you?"

"That's easy." Sharpay snapped her fingers. "The best writer in class – Kelsi Neilsen."

"Kelsi?" Ryan repeated with a frown. "But she's written the lyrics for an entire musical. She doesn't need you to help her write one poem. How are you going to get her to collaborate with you?"

"My dear brother," Sharpay replied, "I have my ways. Trust me."

* * *

By lunch period, Troy was feeling frustrated. All morning, he'd been trying to find the perfect poetry subject from his everyday life. He didn't have a lot of luck. He only hoped Chad, Zeke and Jason were busting rhymes like crazy.

When Troy approached their lunch table, however, he didn't hear anything close to poetry talk. Chad and Zeke were talking basketball.

"That play was awesome, dude!" Jason cried.

Chad jumped to his feet and strutted around the table. "I faked left, then right, then I circled the dude, right–"

"And there was Troy, under the basket," Zeke yelled.

"A simple handoff and we won the game!" Jason roared.

Chad laughed and banged the table. "I think those guys at City Central are still watching the instant replay and trying to figure out what we did and how we did it."

Zeke nodded. "I told Coach Bolton he ought to

try that play again in our next game."

Chad shook his head. "Dude, you can't repeat magic. It just happens."

"Guys," Troy said, sitting down beside them. "You're talking b-ball again. But if you're going to keep playing, you all have to come up with a poem for Ms Barrington's class. And the clock is ticking."

"Dude, lighten up," said Chad. "There's no harm in talking about basketball a little."

"Yeah, don't worry so much, Troy," Zeke replied. "I haven't forgotten the lessons from last night."

"Neither have I," Jason said. "All morning, I've been trying to find inspiration. You know, in my ordinary life."

"That's great," Troy said. "I have, too. So what have you come up with?"

Jason shrugged. "I guess my life is a little too ordinary, because I got nothin'."

"Word," said Chad. "I started out writing a poem about that soapy chemical smell in the bus."

Troy nodded. "That's the spirit."

Chad shook his head. "I missed my stop."

Jason stared glumly at the food on his tray. He fingered a Tater Tot, dipped it in ketchup, and shoved it into his mouth. "Guess we just don't have the right stuff to be poets," he said between chews.

"Yeah," Chad agreed. "That's what I was trying to tell you dudes yesterday."

"Well, I disagree," Zeke said. "I mean, just look at this beautiful Tater Tot." He held one up. "I bet I can come up with a poem right now, just looking at it."

Chad snorted. "I'll take that bet."

Zeke stood up. He held the Tater Tot up to the sunlight streaming in through the cafeteria window. Some kids sitting at tables nearby took notice. They listened in as Zeke began to recite:

"Oh, Tater Tot, oh, Tater Tot, so tiny and round,
What an amazing potato taste in you I have
   found!

Crispy on the outside, soft and mushy inside –
What kind of mysterious potato do you hide?
Russet, white, Yukon gold or Idaho?
Are you mashed or baked or fried – I really
    don't know!
Mystery spud, so tasty and round,
What an amazing lunchtime treat in you I have
    found."

Everyone at the table applauded, and Zeke bowed. The kids around him clapped and whooped and laughed.

"That's pretty funny, Chef Zeke," said Chad. "But if you recite something like that for class, I don't know what grade Ms Barrington's going to give you."

"At least he came up with something," Jason countered. "Some of us are still tongue-tied."

"See what I mean," Troy said. "You guys are spending too much time talking and thinking about basketball. Focus on your poetry!"

Jason stood up. "I can do this. I know I can.

69

I think I've actually got something."

"That's the spirit," said Troy. "Go ahead."

Jason nodded and began to speak:

"When I'm feeling down and kind of crazy,
I come down here to the cafeteria lady,
Sloppy joes, burgers, fries and spaghetti,
When I have a problem, she make me
forget-ee."

Some groans came from the next table.

"What?" Jason asked, blinking blankly. "What's wrong with that poem?"

"Sorry to break the bad news," said Chad, "but there's no such word as 'forget-ee'."

"Okay, so I made it up," Jason confessed defensively. "But, dude, admit it. The word *sounds* poetic."

Though they didn't feel inspired themselves, the Wildcats' rhymes were inspiring kids at the other tables. Soon dozens of students were clowning around, reciting schoolhouse poetry.

THE EYE OF THE BEHOLDER

They say that beauty is only skin deep, but I actually think the opposite is true. Take someone like Gabriella. She doesn't use a lot of makeup or girlie accessories and she doesn't spend a fortune on her wardrobe. Even if you never got to know her you would think she was really pretty, but you only have to be around her for a few minutes to realize that what really makes her beautiful is her personality and confidence. If you ask me, the best kind of beauty starts inside the skin!

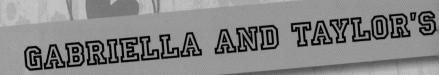

GABRIELLA AND TAYLOR'S

Gabriella and Taylor are both known for being natural beauties. BUT EVEN THEY CAN'T PULL IT OFF WITHOUT A LITTLE WORK AND CARE!

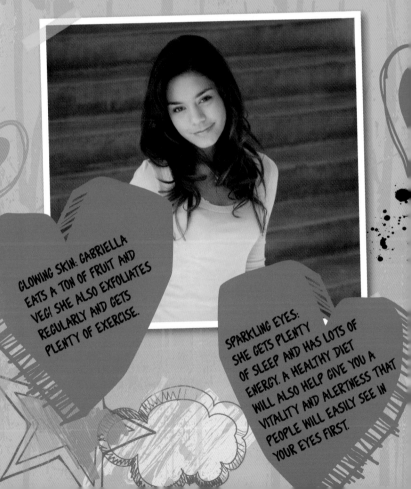

GLOWING SKIN: GABRIELLA EATS A TON OF FRUIT AND VEG! SHE ALSO EXFOLIATES REGULARLY AND GETS PLENTY OF EXERCISE.

SPARKLING EYES: SHE GETS PLENTY OF SLEEP AND HAS LOTS OF ENERGY. A HEALTHY DIET WILL ALSO HELP GIVE YOU A VITALITY AND ALERTNESS THAT PEOPLE WILL EASILY SEE IN YOUR EYES FIRST.

BEAUTY SECRETS

SHINY HAIR: TAYLOR DOESN'T USE A LOT OF TREATMENTS THAT DAMAGE HAIR AND SHE IS KEEN TO USE THE RIGHT KIND OF CONDITIONER. PLUS, SHE HAS A RITUAL OF USING A SPECIAL TREATMENT MADE SPECIFICALLY FOR HER HAIR TYPE EVERY COUPLE OF WEEKS TO GIVE HER HAIR THAT LOVELY GLOSS AND BODY.

LUSCIOUS LIPS: EVER THE PRAGMATIST, TAYLOR NEVER GOES ANYWHERE WITHOUT LIP SALVE AND LIP GLOSS IN HER HANDBAG.

SHARPAY'S
BEAUTY SALON

Here are a few of Sharpay's top tips about always looking your best (OR DISGUISE YOURSELF WHEN YOU CAN'T!)

Face Pack Recipe:
15ml of natural yoghurt (not non-fat or low-fat)
15ml of runny honey (you might need to heat it slightly)

Mix the yoghurt and honey together and apply to the face (be careful not to get any in your eyes, just in case they are sensitive); let sit for 15 minutes; wash off with warm water and towel dry

Tips for bad hair days: A hat will always work in an emergency. Since you never know when you might have a bad hair day it pays to have a lot of hats to match your outfits.

Tip for nice eyes: Put cucumbers on them for 15 minutes to reduce any swelling.
Tip for eye bags: If you're all out of cucumbers and wake up with big bags, shades can still save the day. Again, better stock up on a variety of shades to accessorize your outfits and hats!

HSM HAIR STYLES

There are almost as many hairstyles at East High as students! Read about a few of them and think about ways you could alter your style.

Gabriella prefers a CUTE AND GIRLIE look to her hair. She pulls this off by putting her hair in fun plaits or pulling it back with a really cute hair slide.

1. LOOSELY PART YOUR HAIR IN THE MIDDLE AND SEPARATE INTO TWO BUNCHES
2. PLAIT EACH BUNCH AND SECURE AT THE END WITH A BAND
3. LET A FEW STRANDS OF HAIR FALL DOWN THE SIDES OF YOUR FACE. OR CLIP THEM BACK WITH A PRETTY SLIDE

Taylor's hair often looks SASSY, but she still likes to keep it simple. You'll often see her walking the halls with a funky Alice band with cool patterns and her hair straight down.

1. COMB YOUR HAIR WHEN IT'S WET
2. PUT ON A FUNKY ALICE BAND, PULLING SOME LOCKS OF HAIR FORWARD AT THE SIDES OF YOUR FACE
3. USING A LITTLE BIT OF GEL OR MOUSSE, CURL THE HAIR AT THE SIDE OF YOUR FACE AROUND YOUR FINGERS UNTIL IT HOLDS IN SASSY RINGLETS

SHARPAY HAS MORE HAIR STYLES THAN THE REST OF EAST HIGH PUT TOGETHER! Sometimes her hair is sophisticated with a high ponytail and fringe. Other times she accents her hair with an elaborate head scarf that never fails to catch the eye!

1. COMB A LARGE SECTION OF HAIR FROM THE TOP OF YOUR HEAD FORWARD TO SEPARATE IT FROM THE REST, THEN BRUSH THE REST OF YOUR HAIR SMOOTH AND FIX IT INTO A PONYTAIL WITH A SMALL HAIR BAND
2. COMB THE FRONT SECTION TO THE SIDE, SCOOPING ACROSS YOUR FOREHEAD, AND CLIP IT IN PLACE
3. FINISH THE LOOK WITH A FANCY SCARF TIED AROUND THE SMALL HAIR BAND

COLOUR MAGIC

The colours you choose to wear can SAY A LOT ABOUT YOU. Sometimes they can bring out the best in you and really reflect your personality. Other times they just clash with your hair, skin tone, eyes or don't seem to suit you at all (but that's what friends are for – to tell you these things!)

Gabriella often chooses cool colours that are soft and neutral and tend not to attract any undue attention. She prefers whites and pastels.

Taylor typically likes colours that are warm and earthy. She prefers brown, dark blue, gray and black.

As you might expect, Sharpay likes colours that are dramatic and have a lot of flash and flair. She prefers bright red, gold, silver and pink.

There was an ode to study hall, a sonnet about chemistry lab, a haiku about field trips. There was even an epic poem that told the story of a heinously difficult woodwork project.

Sitting with some of the other members of the Scholastic Decathlon team, quiet, studious Martha Cox heard snatches of the lunchtime poetry. Her ears instantly pricked up.

"What's going on?" she asked, her eyes bright.

Betty Hong closed her book and leaned close. "Taylor McKessie told me all about it," she whispered. Betty told Martha about next week's poetry-reading assembly and how Taylor was trying to help half the starting basketball team locate their muse.

"That's totally fresh!" Martha cried. "Too bad I'm not in Ms Barrington's English class."

Betty made a face. "You like that poetry stuff? I thought you were into maths and science."

"I like it all," Martha replied. "I love astronomy *and* hip-hop—"

Betty rolled her eyes. "Not hip-hop again."

"Word, girl," Martha replied. "You know I've been bustin' out kickin' rhymes for years. It helps me remember lessons, like last night's astronomy lecture."

"No," Betty said. "You *didn't* make up a rap to that."

"Just watch," Martha cried. Leaping out of her chair, she began to chant, freestyle:

"At the centre of our system is the molten sun,
A star that burns hot, Fahrenheit two billion
 and one.
But the sun, he ain't alone in the heavenly
 sphere,
He's got nine homeys in orbit, some far,
 some near.
Old Mercury's crowding in 'bout as close
 as he can,
Yo, Merc's a tiny planet who loves a tan. . . .

Some kids around Martha heard her rap. They

really got into it, jumping up from their tables to clap and dance. The beat was contagious. Martha started bustin' some moves herself. She kept the rap flowing, and more kids joined the party. . . .

"Venus is next. She's a real hot planet,
Shrouded by clouds, hot enough to melt granite.
Earth is the third planet from the sun,
Just enough light and heat to make living fun.
Then comes Mars, a planet funky and red.
Covered with sand, the place is pretty dead.
Jupiter's huge! The largest planet of all!
Saturn's big, too, but Uranus is small.
So far away, the place is almost forgotten,
Neptune's view of Earth is pretty rotten.
And last but not least, Pluto's in a fog,
Far away and named after Mickey's home dog.
Yo, that's all the planets orbiting our sun,
But the Milky Way galaxy is far from done!"

When Martha finished her freestyle, hip-hop flow, the entire cafeteria burst into wild applause. Troy, Chad, Zeke, and Jason had been clapping and dancing, too. Now they joined in the whooping and hollering.

"Whoa," said Chad. "Martha's awesome."

CHAPTER SEVEN

Not everyone in the cafeteria thought Martha Cox's rapping was awesome. As Martha took a bow, an envious Sharpay Evans spun on her high-heeled boots and gave the girl her back.

"She's good," her brother Ryan noted.

"I wasn't listening," said Sharpay, flipping back her blonde hair. She marched up the stairs to the cafeteria balcony. Ryan ran to catch up with her.

"Where are you going?" he asked.

"Where you're *not*. So get lost," she commanded.

"Well, I guess *somebody* fell out of the wrong side of the wardrobe this morning!" Ryan snapped before descending the stairs.

Sharpay stomped her foot and suppressed a scream. "How could this happen," she whispered to herself. "How could a pair of geeks like Martha Cox and Taylor McKessie write poems that are better than mine?"

Amazing, but true, it seemed. Sharpay knew she had to do something desperate to beat Taylor – something so extraordinarily pathetic she couldn't believe she was about to do it. But she had no choice.

Sharpay Evans was about to ask, to plead, to beg for help! She scanned the cafeteria tables below her and finally spied Kelsi Neilsen. She was sitting by herself in the corner, scribbling in one of her notebooks.

"Showtime," Sharpay whispered, striding over to the shrimpy Sondheim.

"Hey, Kelsi. How's my favourite composer?" Sharpay said, her smile so wide it was beginning to hurt her face.

Kelsi was surprised, confused and a little suspicious of Sharpay's sudden interest in her. "Er . . . Hi, Sharpay. Can I help you?"

"I was just thinking that since I'm always the girl in the limelight, it might be wise to let a little of the light shine on those less . . . gifted."

"Uh-huh," Kelsi said.

"I was wondering," Sharpay said, trying to sound casual, "have you started your poem for next week's assembly?"

"Not yet," said Kelsi.

"Well, I spoke with Ms Barrington," Sharpay said, "and she agreed that I could collaborate with someone. In fact, she thought the idea of a collaborative poem was brilliant."

"I see," said Kelsi, leaning back and folding her arms. "In other words, you're totally out of your league and stuck for a poem. Right?"

"Yes." Sharpay groaned and collapsed into the

chair next to Kelsi. "I've done everything. I've picked the perfect ensemble to wear. I've taken voice lessons, drama classes, modelling. I'm the full package. All I need is some words strung together to recite and I'm golden!"

Sharpay closed her mouth, realizing too late that she'd said too much. "Look," she continued. "If you collaborate with me on this assignment, then I'll be happy to do you a favour in return."

Kelsi frowned. "I don't know. . . ."

"Really, you can name it. I'll do anything!" Sharpay cried. Then she quickly added, "Within reason, of course. I'm not doing your laundry or washing your family's car or anything gross like that. *Yuck*. And just because we're collaborators, it doesn't mean we're friends – or even equals."

To Sharpay's surprise, Kelsi smiled. "If you want me to name it, I'm ready."

Sharpay frowned. "Now you're scaring me."

"This weekend, I planned on surprising my grandmother for her birthday," she explained.

"Good so far," Sharpay said.

"I wrote some special songs, just for her. And I was going to play them on the piano during her party at the nursing home, where my grandmother lives," Kelsi continued. "But the nurse who was going to sing them just called me this morning. She's got laryngitis."

Sharpay frowned. "So you want me to sing to a bunch of old people in an old-people's home?"

Kelsi nodded. "They would so love it! You have such a strong voice—"

"I do, don't I?"

"So that's my favour. If you sing the songs that I wrote for my grandmother, then I'll agree to collaborate with you on a poem."

"And when exactly is this party?" she asked.

"Saturday morning," said Kelsi.

"Oh . . ." Sharpay shook her head. "Well, that's an issue because my Saturday mornings are booked. I've got jazz dance and then voice coaching classes, not to mention Pilates!"

Disappointed, Kelsi shrugged. "I guess I'll just have to ask Gabriella then. I'll bet she'll do it. Or maybe I'll talk to Taylor McKessie. You never know, one of them might want to collaborate on a poem, too—"

"No!" Sharpay quickly cried. "I'll be *happy* to sing for granny."

"Then I'll be happy to collaborate with you." Kelsi smiled and held out her hand. "I'm sure this will work out great for both of us."

"Yeah . . . great," Sharpay replied, shaking Kelsi's small hand. *Or it will be,* she thought, *once I see my picture in the paper!*

After school, Troy was hanging with his friends on the front steps when Gabriella approached them. Troy rose with a smile to greet her.

"Just the person I wanted to see," he said.

Gabriella didn't reply. She'd managed to avoid Troy all day. Now she reached into her pack and pulled out his notebook – the one with the poem gushing about the girl named Ariel.

"You left this at my house last night," Gabriella told him.

"Thanks." Troy tucked the notebook under his arm. "And thanks again for all your help last night. In fact, I was wondering if you could help us again tonight? The guys are making some progress. But they're not across the finishing line yet. Maybe if you listen to some of the stuff they're coming up with, you could help?"

As he spoke, Gabriella's frown deepened. She shifted her gaze, refusing to meet his eyes. "I'm sorry, Troy. I can't help you out tonight. I'm supposed to help my mother with a clothing drive at the community centre. She made the commitment weeks ago, and I promised to help her. I really am sorry. Explain to the guys for me, okay?"

"I understand," Troy said. "Maybe I can call you later. . . . Or you can call me? After you get back?"

Gabriella nodded. "Maybe . . . although I'm not sure when I'll be home." She shrugged.

"Sure. Okay," said Troy.

She glanced at her watch. "I really have to go."

Troy could tell that something was bothering Gabriella. He was about to ask her what was up, but he didn't get a chance. Before he could open his mouth again, she quickly turned and walked away.

Chad saw the entire exchange. As Gabriella vanished around the corner, he put his hand on Troy's shoulder. "Brrrr," he said, pretending to shiver. "Did it just get cold in here, or what?"

Troy shrugged and tried to mask his disappointment. "She's just busy tonight, that's all. I'll talk to her again tomorrow."

But Troy couldn't hide his true feelings from his best friend. Chad could see the hurt and confusion behind his eyes. It seemed like Gabriella was upset with him for some reason. But he couldn't imagine why.

"Come on," Troy said. "Let's get back to work. We have to write poems, with or without Gabriella's help."

Gabriella gritted her teeth as she walked away.

She felt so many emotions right now – anger, hurt, humiliation.

She'd wanted to confront Troy about this Ariel person. But she was too embarrassed. If she asked him about his poem, he'd know she had invaded his privacy by reading the papers that fell out of his notebook. Not that it mattered, anyway. It was obvious from the poem how he felt.

"I've just got to face it," Gabriella murmured to herself. "Troy's crushing on some other girl, and she obviously means more to him than I do."

Did this Ariel go to another school? Or live in another city? Or state?

"I know Troy likes me," Gabriella whispered. But she also knew that some boys liked juggling two or more girlfriends at a time. She just never thought Troy Bolton was that type of guy. Clearly, he was. And Gabriella was devastated.

"I can't believe I misjudged him so badly. . . ."

CHAPTER EIGHT

After school, Troy gathered his team-mates in a corner of the playground across the street from the high school. He hoped they'd each come up with a brilliant poem to recite. Instead, they kept coming up empty.

Finally Chad tossed a basketball to Troy and threw up his hands. "I've never quit anything in my life," he said. "But I'm ready to quit this poetry thing right now. I'd rather throw in the towel than risk total schoolwide embarrassment."

Troy caught the ball and faked to Jason before bounce-passing it to Zeke.

"Man . . . you . . . got . . . that . . . right," Zeke said, punctuating each word with a dribble. Then he slipped around Troy and slammed the ball through the basket.

Jason ran below to catch it. "Making . . . rhymes is . . . a waste . . . of time," he announced, following each metered beat with a rebound off the backboard.

"But that's a *good* rhyme!" shouted a girl's voice.

The guys turned to find Martha Cox watching them through the fence. She had a pile of school-books in her arms and an MP3 player dangling from her ears.

"You heard that?" Troy asked.

"My MC Dibs song ended, and I was about to hit repeat," Martha said. "Then I heard Jason. What he said sounded like hip-hop poetry to me. Especially with the beat of that bouncing basket-ball."

Troy blinked in surprise. "You're kidding?"

"Word, my man!" Martha replied. "Go for it, Jason. Try it again."

For a long moment, Jason stood quietly with the ball in his hand. Then, face twisted into a painful grimace, he agonized over each word while he spoke it.

"Er . . . Ah," Jason stammered. "It's fun . . . to run . . . in the sun. How's that?"

Martha shook her head. She came around the fence and onto the playground court. "Dribble the ball, move around, try a few layups when you rhyme. Forget your head! Let your heart kick in."

"Man, forget it," Chad said with a dismissive wave.

Martha ignored Chad's words. "Go on, Jason," she insisted. "Try again. You did it once. I know you can do it again."

Jason nodded and began to toss the ball from hand to hand. Then he dribbled around the court. Soon he was playing a mock game. He faked right, dodged left, circled the basket, dribbling the whole time. Then Jason began to rhyme:

"In school and at home, I'm just a nice guy,
But on the court, look out – I'll make you cry!"

Jason completed his rhyme by dunking the ball through the net and hanging on the basket.

Martha laughed. Chad, Zeke and Troy whooped and cheered.

"Man, that worked! What's your secret, Jason?" Chad cried.

Jason dropped to the ground and thought it over.

"I don't have any secret," he said. "It feels like the words just flowed right out of my mouth, without me even trying."

"The words came easily because you were rhyming about something you *love* to do," Martha explained. "Something that brings out the best in you."

Chad blinked. "But Taylor told us to just keep

it simple, write about everyday things. So we tried stuff like cafeteria food, woodwork class, the school bus, tutor group . . ."

Martha shook her head. "Writing about things around you is great, but poetry should never be about things you don't really care about. What's the point of that? Poetry has to mean something to you or it's worthless."

At that moment, something finally clicked inside all the boys. Chad considered her words, then nodded. Jason smiled the way he did when he passed a difficult test. Zeke was grinning like he'd made a perfect crème brûlée.

"Martha's right! Let's all give it a try." Troy snatched the basketball from the ground and dribbled it around the court. Once he made a complete circle, he dribbled it right down the centre of the court, and some rhymes about how much he loved playing basketball began to flow out.

He passed the ball to Chad, then Zeke. Each of them, in turn, came up with more lines.

Martha's words lit a fire under the whole

group. Now Troy knew what they should do. "Let's perform the poem as a team," he said. "We'll take the basketball right onstage and use the bounce to set the rhythm."

"Yeah!" Chad cried. "We'll each recite a stanza. And we can pass the basketball to each other, just like we did here."

"Right!" said Troy. "Each dude who gets the ball takes a turn reciting a part of our poem."

"But we'll need something to start the poem," Zeke said. "Lines of poetry to connect our solos."

"And an ending, too," said Jason.

All eyes turned to Martha Cox.

"You don't need me to figure all that out," she said, blushing. "You're on your way."

"Don't leave now!" Troy cried. "This was your idea, and you can't just abandon us. You've got to listen to what we come up with and tell us if we're on track."

"And help us with the choreography–" Chad said.

"And the moves–" Jason added.

"Dude, get a dictionary," Chad said. "Choreography *is* the moves!"

"Well, we need Martha for both, right?" Jason replied.

"We do." Troy faced Martha. "We need you. Will you help us?"

"Sure," she replied.

Chad, Zeke and Jason ran over to her, grabbed the pile of books in her arms and placed them safely on a nearby bench. Then they ran back onto the playground court like they were getting ready to start a game.

"Okay, Wildcats!" Troy yelled, clapping his hands and moving onto the court with them. "Let's get to work!"

That same night, when Gabriella got home from the charity work, she automatically picked up her mobile phone to call Troy. She wanted to talk to him and tell him about her evening. But then she remembered his "Ariel" poem and she put down the phone.

In five days, in front of the whole school, Troy was going to recite a love poem about some girl named Ariel.

"And what am I going to read?" Gabriella murmured.

She crossed the bedroom and picked up her English notebook. Inside, she'd already started her poem. It was all about Troy and how great she thought he was. But how could she read a poem about Troy when he was going to read a poem about some other girl? It was just too humiliating.

Gabriella ripped the poem out of her notebook, crumpled it up, and threw it away. "I'd better write about something else," she whispered. "Like . . . a pretty garden."

She closed her eyes and tried to picture flowers and leaves, sunlight and earth. An hour later, she had five stanzas. "Springtime Garden," she wrote at the top of the page.

The poem's rhyme scheme and meter were perfect. It talked of smells and colours, petals and dewdrops – and it had absolutely no life at all.

The lines were pretty, but they were empty.

Once again, Gabriella ripped the page out of her notebook and crumpled it up. The poems she admired the most were about powerful things – love and loss, joy and sorrow, beauty and pain.

Gabriella knew those poems were powerful for a good reason. The poets were writing about things that really mattered to them.

Turning to a clean page, Gabriella lifted her pencil again. She closed her eyes and asked herself what was in her heart, right at this moment. She thought about Troy and her discovery. She thought about her pain and confusion. And then she began to write. . . .

Three days later, Kelsi Neilsen was ready to tear her hair out. *Arrrgh*, she thought. Writing with Sharpay is a total nightmare!

By now, the weekend had come and gone. Sharpay had held up her end of the bargain. She'd sung like an angel at the nursing-home party for Kelsi's grandmother.

So naturally Kelsi felt obligated to hold up her end of the deal. But Sharpay was driving Kelsi bonkers. She'd insisted on taking control of the project and her ideas were awful!

First, she'd instructed Kelsi to write a poem about her favourite handbags. After two stanzas about clasps, straps and zippered pouches, Sharpay changed her mind, crumpled up the paper and declared, "Let's do the joys of shopping instead."

Kelsi gave her stanzas about the bright lights of department stores, the buzz of the crowds, the lines at the register. Then Sharpay changed her mind *again*.

"Let's focus on me instead," she decided.

Next came a haiku about Sharpay's voice. She said the poem was too short. Then came an ode to the beauty of her feet.

"This isn't working, either!" Sharpay complained, pacing her bedroom. She balled up the paper with Kelsi's opening stanzas and threw it down on the carpet.

There were now so many crumpled poems littering the floor, Sharpay's bedroom looked like a winter wonderland of paper snowballs.

Driven nearly insane, Kelsi stood and threw up her hands. "I've had it!" she cried. "I quit!"

"You can't quit," Sharpay calmly replied. "We had a deal. And I held up *my* end of it."

"But your ideas are ridiculous!" Kelsi told her. "You need to get real!"

Sharpay had been pacing back and forth. Now she stood stock-still. She met Kelsi's eyes. "The truth is . . ." she admitted in a quiet voice. "I don't know how to do that."

Kelsi sunk back down into the desk chair. She surveyed the crumpled papers blanketing the floor and sighed. "Listen, Sharpay, I won't quit on you. But for this to be a true collaboration, then we need to start working *together*."

"I thought we were working together."

"No," said Kelsi. "You were selecting the subject and ordering me how to write the poem. We're going to try something different now."

Sharpay's eyes narrowed skeptically. "What?"

"You're going to write a stanza, then I'll write one," said Kelsi. "We'll alternate."

Sharpay shrugged. "You know . . . I've actually already written one stanza. It's on my laptop. But Ryan said it was tragically bad."

"Why don't you show it to me," Kelsi suggested.

Sharpay walked over to her desk and fired up her laptop. Kelsi read the single stanza onscreen about Sharpay's shoes.

"It's not really bad," Kelsi said. "In fact, I'd say it's a pretty good start."

"Really?" Sharpay asked.

"Really," said Kelsi. "Now let's *both* start writing. . . ."

CHAPTER NINE

The day of the special assembly finally came. One by one, the members of Ms Barrington's English class delivered their poems.

Most of the students wrote about the expected subjects – landscapes and rainbows, a favourite pet, a singing sparrow, that sort of thing. They all received polite applause.

Gabriella was standing in the wings. She was up next, and she couldn't get her nerves under control. Troy hadn't read his poem about Ariel yet, and she was dreading it. She didn't know how she would take the whispers and the gossip – or her own heartache.

She forced herself to focus on Taylor McKessie, now at the microphone, reciting a long poem about a winter's day. The poem contained a lot of complicated metaphors – some about the geometry of snowflakes, others about the way "the pendant mass" of icicles formed during a frigid night.

Taylor was presenting interesting images, and she was doing a good job painting word pictures. But during Taylor's recitation, Gabriella couldn't stop her mind from wandering.

I guess I'm too nervous to concentrate, she decided when she caught herself staring off into space.

Finally, Taylor finished, and Ms Barrington strode across the stage. "How about a hand for Taylor's brilliant poem, 'The Ice Storm Cometh'?" she declared.

The kids politely applauded, and Ms

Barrington grinned with pride. "Taylor's mix of pentameter and dimeter iambic lines was perfect, a textbook example of a Ronsardian ode!"

Taylor smiled. "Thank you, Ms Barrington," she said and strode offstage.

"And now, we have our next poet." Ms Barrington glanced at Gabriella in the wings and nodded. "Gabriella Montez."

Gabriella swallowed nervously. She wiped a wet palm on her green velvet skirt and forced herself to stop gripping her notebook page so tightly.

As she walked toward the standing microphone, a bright white spotlight nearly blinded her. She could only make out the first few rows of seats. But she'd seen the assembly hall before the houselights were lowered and she knew the place was packed.

Don't think about that. Think about something else, she quietly told herself. But what? For a moment she closed her eyes. That's when she knew what to do.

Just pretend you're reading the poem to one person, she told herself. Just pretend you're reading to Troy.

She cleared her throat and began with the title.

"Honesty," she announced.

Her slightly shaky voice echoed through the dark assembly hall. The single word and the long silence after it made the students in the audience sit up a little straighter in their seats. Then Gabriella began to recite:

"I see you there in front of me—
Your face, your hands, your eyes.
I hear you talk, I hear you tell
Your hopes, your dreams, your lies.

I walked with you, a sunlit trail,
Together hand in hand.
Then twilight came, and you were gone,
And now alone I stand.

The woods are cold, the trees are black,
The dark is closing in.
And you have gone away from me,
Your faultless light has dimmed.

Betrayal is an empty space,
Raw night, cold room, alone.
And no one can redeem your face,
Sweet knight, safe light, you're gone."

As Gabriella finished the last line, she swallowed and tilted her head back. Tears had welled up in her eyes, and she didn't want any to spill over. She didn't want Troy to see her crying.

The entire audience sat staring in complete silence. But this wasn't like the silence at the end of everyone else's poem. There was no shuffling of feet, no whispers, no mumbling. This silence was different.

"Thank you," Gabriella finally said.

A moment later, without Ms Barrington prompting them, the entire assembly hall ripped into loud, sustained applause.

Gabriella stepped back, a little stunned by the force of it. Then she nodded uncertainly and ran off the stage, passing Ms Barrington on her way out.

"Very nice, Gabriella," Ms Barrington said when the applause died down. "Thank you for your honesty. And now we move on to our final poems of the day. These last two poems were written as rengas. Traditionally, this is a form of poetry in which more than one poet participates."

She motioned to the wings for Sharpay and Kelsi to step out. "And now for our first renga," announced the teacher, "here are Sharpay Evans and Kelsi Neilsen with their poem, 'Step by Step'."

Sharpay strutted out with a beaming grin, wearing a sparkly silver dress and a glittering pair of high heels.

Kelsi followed with her head down, clearly nervous. Her outfit was the complete opposite of Sharpay's – cargo pants, combat boots and a flannel shirt.

Together they moved to the standing microphone. Then Sharpay gave a high kick and her
voice boomed out:

"Shoes, shoes, how I love them.
Let me count the styles,
Mules, pumps, slippers, slingbacks,
Leathers and crocodiles . . ."

Kelsi's quiet voice came next:

"March, march, always steady,
Through rain and sleet and snow.
Boots, thick, solid, sturdy,
That's the sole I show. . . ."

Sharpay did a few dance moves and crooned,

"Heel, toe, step, ball-chain,
Legs lighter than air.
Tap, jazz, ballet, ballroom,
Dance without a care . . ."

Kelsi spoke:

"Stride, stride, every morning,
Through my day I move.
Streets, curbs, lawns and gardens,
I push, I strive, I rove. . . ."

The girls continued to alternate stanzas until the very last one. "Feet, feet, always moving," Sharpay recited. "But can you tell me why?"

"The path you take is yours to make," Kelsi said. "Don't let life pass you by."

The moment they finished, the auditorium broke out into spirited applause. A few kids even whistled and cheered to show how much they liked the poem.

Sharpay was thrilled. She looked down at Kelsi, took her hand and raised it up.

"Big finish?" she whispered.

Kelsi nodded and together the girls took a deep, theatrical bow.

"Wonderful! Just wonderful!" Ms Barrington

was clapping as she came back out onstage. "And now for our final poem, we have another collaborative effort. Here are Troy Bolton, Chad Danforth, Zeke Baylor and Jason Cross to perform 'Poetry in Motion.'"

The boys came out as a team, dressed in their Wildcats uniforms. Using tightly coordinated basketball moves, they passed the ball as they moved across the stage.

Then Troy began to dribble the ball, keeping a steady beat. He bounced the ball lower and lower, the other boys bending low with him. Finally, they began to recite:

"On the ground
We are bound,
We are lower than down.

But the sound
Of the ball
Bouncing small, growing tall,

As they recited, they lifted themselves up higher and higher until they were standing straight again.

Helps us move
To a groove
And a beat we approve.

Before long,
We're bouncing
Up higher than the sky.

Before long,
We're soaring,
Defying gravity."

Troy passed the ball to Jason Cross, who kept dribbling with a steady beat and began to recite solo:

"In school and at home, I'm just a nice guy,
But on the court, look out, I'll make you cry!

I'll slip and slide, I'll ice you out.
No, you can't touch me, that's without a doubt.
Slip move, duck right, layup, rebound,
On the court, my feet don't touch the ground."

Jason passed the ball to Zeke. Then Zeke began to dribble and recite.

"Cooking's my thing, in the kitchen or court,
Laugh if you want 'cause I'm a good sport!
Don't mess with me when I got the ball,
'Cause you'll be heading for a mighty fall.
Fiery hot, no one can stand my heat.
When I'm in the game, all others look beat."

Zeke shot the ball to Chad, who immediately began to dribble and rhyme.

"In homeroom and in class, yeah all around,
Everyone knows me as the high school clown.
Sure I like a good joke of any sort,
But my clowning ends when I'm on the court.

There it's all business, and I'm something more,
Ain't no one better when I want to score!"

With a broad smile, Chad confidently passed the ball to Troy. This is going great, Troy thought. And we're almost home. . . .

"I'm captain of the team, and it's intense.
Before the game, I want to hop the fence.
Then the whistle blows, and I'm in the game.
That single sound melts down my doubt
     and shame.
The change complete, I'm king of every court,
Me and my team, we never come up short."

Next Troy passed the ball around to all his friends. From Jason to Zeke to Chad and back to Troy again. Then all the boys began to chant:

"On the ground
We are bound,
We are lower than down.

Before long,
We're bouncing
Up, higher than the sky.

Before long,
We're soaring,
Defying gravity.

Through the air,
Not one care,
Yeah, this feeling is rare.

Through the air,
Not one care,
Yeah, this feeling is rare.
Through the air, not one care!"

By the middle of "Poetry in Motion," all the students in the auditorium were on their feet, clapping to the poem's driving rhythm. By the end, the place went crazy. The kids were hooting, hollering, cheering, and clapping.

Backstage, Ms Barrington heard the explosion. She turned to the drama teacher and raised an eyebrow. "Well," she said, "I'm not the one judging this contest. But it seems to me we already have four winners."

"Indeed we do," Ms Darbus agreed, adding her own applause to the thunder. "Indeed we do!"

CHAPTER TEN

Five minutes later, Ms Barrington was back in front of the assembly, unfolding a piece of paper. "And now I'd like to announce today's awards."

She opened the piece of paper and declared. "Honourable mention goes to 'The Ice Storm Cometh' by Taylor McKessie!"

The audience politely clapped.

"The third-place certificate goes to 'Step by Step' by Sharpay Evans and Kelsi Neilsen."

The audience clapped louder.

Backstage, Kelsi smiled. "Third place, not bad."

Sharpay sighed. "It's not first, and that is disappointing. But I did beat Taylor – *and* I was awesome!"

Kelsi rolled her eyes, and Ms Barrington continued announcing the awards. "The second-place certificate goes to 'Honesty' by Gabriella Montez. . . ."

Gabriella was stunned – not only by the award and the loud applause, but by the fact that Troy still hadn't read that poem about his crush-girl – Ariel.

"And last but far from least, we have the first-place ribbon for East High's poetry assembly. But the winner will not be announced by me. For that, I'd like to bring out our special guest judge, the accomplished, award-winning poet, Mr Julius Ibsen!"

A heavyset African-American man strode onto the stage. As soon as the kids saw him they began to whisper and murmur.

Julius Ibsen looked very familiar to them – and for a very good reason. "Hey, there, kids," his deep voice boomed out. "It's very nice to be with you this afternoon. You have some very talented classmates, and it's been a pleasure spending time listening to their creative efforts."

"You the man, Dibs!" someone shouted from the back of the room.

Julius Ibsen smiled. "I see someone's recognized me." He laughed. "Well, I guess that's all right. Julius Donald Ibsen isn't the only name I write under. Many of you may know me better by the name I use in the recording industry: MC Dibs."

The kids in the assembly hall started clapping and hooting. Most of them were huge fans of hip-hop recordings written and produced by the man standing right in front of them.

"You see, I met your English teacher, Ms Barrington, while I was earning my degree in fine arts. I learned a lot in school, and I can see Ms Barrington's doing a fine job with all of you. Now let's get to that winning poem!"

The kids clapped.

"The winner is not only going to be published in the local paper. I've decided to use their lyrics on the next album I produce. And that honor I bestow to–"

Dibs glanced down at his piece of paper to make sure he read all of the names correctly. "Troy Bolton, Chad Danforth, Zeke Baylor and Jason Cross for 'Poetry in Motion'!"

Backstage, Troy and his friends stood in stunned silence for a second. Ms Barrington rushed over to them. "Congratulations, boys!" she cried. "Now go out there and get your picture taken with Julius!"

The boys bounded out to more applause, hoots and whistles. They shook hands with MC Dibs and Troy held their first-place ribbon high. But just before the photographer snapped their photo, the boys stopped him.

"Hold up a second," Chad said. Then he dashed offstage, found Martha Cox in the audience and pulled the blushing hip-hop-loving girl into the picture, too.

"Nice going, Chad," Taylor told him a few minutes later.

"Thanks," he said. "It's a pretty cool feeling, I have to admit."

"And not a split leotard in sight," she added with a wink.

Chad rolled his eyes. "Let's not go there."

"Anyway, you did great."

Chad gestured to her honourable mention certificate. "You did, too."

"No . . ." Taylor shook her head. "My poem wasn't bad or anything. It had perfect meter and rhyme, but . . ." She smiled and shrugged. "It never came alive. Not like 'Poetry in Motion'. And art has to be real to be good."

"Yeah," Chad agreed. "It does."

"It's hard to believe," she said, "but you and your basketball buddies have actually taught me something today."

Chad laughed. "Well, don't worry, Ms Brainiac. We won't let it go to our heads."

"Hey, you got second place," Troy said, walking up to Gabriella backstage.

She nodded and looked down at the certificate. "It's a surprise. I didn't expect it. I really just wrote the poem for me . . . to express my feelings."

Troy nodded. "Your poem was really powerful," he said. And he meant it, too. He knew Gabriella's poem was about betrayal, about how someone she'd trusted had let her down. Troy wondered who had hurt Gabriella and how. But with half the English class around them talking excitedly, Troy knew this wasn't the time or place for a discussion like that.

"Congratulations," she told him.

Troy frowned. Her voice was cold when she spoke and she wouldn't even look at him.

"Gabriella, what's the matter?" he asked.

"Nothing," she said. "I've got to go."

She started to walk away. Then she stopped herself and turned back to face him. "Why didn't you read your other poem? The one about your secret crush?"

Troy's eyes widened. "My what?!"

"Your crush. That girl, Ariel . . ." She confessed that she'd read the poem in his notebook. So there was no reason for him to pretend anymore. "I know you're really into another girl."

Troy stared in disbelief a moment, then shook his head and laughed. "Oh, wow," he said. "I don't believe it. . . ."

Gabriella tensed. She didn't know why Troy was laughing, but she wasn't amused. Feeling embarrassed, she started walking away from him. She needed to get away from the crowd.

"Gabriella!" Troy called as he followed her through the door. "Gabriella, wait!"

Troy caught her arm in the empty hallway. "You don't understand!"

"What don't I understand, Troy?" she snapped.

"Ariel isn't a girl!" he cried. "Ariel was the

name of my skateboard in sixth grade!" Oh, how Troy loved that skateboard. That's what his first poem had been about.

Gabriella blinked. She thought back to the lines she'd read in Troy's notebook. . . .

When I'm down or lonely,
I roll with you and smile.
You take me to the limit.
You lift me Ariel-style!

"Omigosh," she whispered, feeling supreme-ly stupid. "I thought that you . . ." She shook her head.

"You thought I was lying to you?" Troy said. "That I was paying attention to you while I was crushing on some other girl?"

Gabriella nodded.

"Well, let me set the record straight." Troy dug into his pocket and handed her a tightly folded piece of paper.

"What's this?" she asked.

"It's another poem I wrote," he said.

Curious, Gabriella unfolded the paper and scanned the bold handwriting.

For Gabriella
by Troy Bolton

You lift your voice, and I lift mine,
Two bright ribbons intertwine.

I hear the pulse, I feel the beat,
We sing as one, we are complete.

Duets are not for one, but two,
And no one else for me but you.

Gabriella felt her eyes welling up again, but this time for a very different reason. "It's beautiful," she whispered.

Troy smiled. "I thought about reading it for the assembly, but . . ." He shrugged. "The guys needed me."

Gabriella met Troy's eyes. "I understand. And you know what? I'm glad you didn't read this one."

"Really? Why? Is the rhyme scheme off?"

"Not at all, it's a wonderful poem. It's just that . . ." Gabriella paused to think of the right words. "As important as it is for the world to hear your honesty, sometimes a poem can be more private . . . like a shooting star that only two people can see."

Troy smiled and took her hand. "Like you and me."

Something new is on the way!
Look for the next book in the Disney High School Musical: Stories from East High series...

CRUNCH TIME

By N.B. Grace

Based on the Disney Channel Original Movie
"High School Musical", written by Peter Barsocchini

It was only 8:30 in the morning, but an air of nervousness already filled Ms Darbus's tutor room. Gabriella Montez chewed her lip and flipped through her calculus textbook, doing one last-minute check to make sure she had really memorized all the formulas that were going to be on today's big test.

Three rows back, Troy Bolton had his eyes closed, but he wasn't nodding off. Instead, he was mentally going over the new drill that the basketball team had learned two days before. He was going to lead practice today, and he wanted to make extra sure that he knew the moves backwards and forwards.

Two rows over, Sharpay Evans passed her brother Ryan a note with yet another idea about how they could improve the dance routine they were creating for the talent contest – true, it was months away, but it was never too early to start working on perfection! Ryan read the note and then looked over at his sister in awe. Once again, Sharpay had demonstrated why she was destined to be world-famous by the time she was twenty-five. He mouthed the word, "Brilliant!" and she nodded smugly.

Ms Darbus looked out at the class and sighed. She had never seen a more distracted group of students since – well, to be fair, since yesterday's tutor group. She was about to call the class to order when the speaker on the wall emitted a loud screech.

Everyone jumped, even though they should have known this was coming. Principal Matsui was completely incapable of handling any kind of sound system. Every morning started with a painful blast of feedback.

Another loud screech. Troy groaned, Ryan put his head on his desk and Sharpay put her hands over her ears. Ms Darbus rolled her eyes and made a mental note to once again offer to have one of her stagehands teach Principal Matsui the basics of volume control.

Finally, Principal Matsui managed to get his mike to work. His voice boomed out over the PA system.

"Good morning, East High School!" he cried. "It's now time for the morning announcements!"

In the back row, Zeke Baylor let his head fall back against the wall and closed his eyes. Unlike his friends, he wasn't distracted by looming tests, basketball drills or dance routines, and he had found that the morning announcements always offered a good opportunity to get a little shut-eye. After all, so many of them were about totally boring topics, like—

"Remember the SAT tutoring sessions start this week!" the principal said. "They'll be held on Tuesdays and Thursdays for an hour after school and they'll be led by other students! Not only will you learn a lot, but I'm sure that you'll make new friends and have a lot of fun!"

Studying for the SAT – fun?

Zeke opened his eyes just long enough to look over at his friend Chad Danforth with an expression of exaggerated horror. Chad and Zeke had been dreading this test since their freshman year, because most colleges used SAT scores to determine which students would be admitted and, more to the point, which would be rejected. Zeke and Chad got good grades, but the idea of sitting in a room for three hours and taking a test that would decide what colleges they would or would not get into . . . well, that was more pressure than shooting a free throw in the last five seconds of a basketball game!

123

There was no way you could call anything to do with the SATs 'fun', Zeke thought. This was just further evidence for his pet theory that Principal Matsui was actually from a different planet. Possibly a different universe.

"Be sure to sign up in the office as soon as possible, because these sessions are filling up fast!" the principal went on.

Sharpay rolled her eyes. He was starting to sound like one of those desperate salespeople on late-night TV commercials, she thought, the ones who tried to persuade you to buy hair defrizzers and sardine fillet knives.

"So, sign up!" he repeated. "Now!"

There was a long moment of silence as the principal apparently paused for dramatic effect. Gabriella glanced around the room. No one seemed very psyched about the SAT-tutoring sessions.

She sighed. She didn't really want to be a brainiac, but it was in her nature. She couldn't help it – she *did* think that trying to get a high

SAT score would be kind of fun. It was a contest, just like trying to win a basketball game or to get the lead in a school play, and no one thought *those* competitions were boring. . . .

Her thoughts were interrupted by Principal Matsui, who had finally reached the last announcement of the day.

"And now, I have one final and very exciting bit of news!" His voice boomed from the PA speaker. "The Student Council has decided on the theme for this year's Halloween Festival, and I think it's one that every student will enjoy. The theme is 'Future Fantasy'. Everyone is invited to come to the festival dressed as the person they think they'll be in twenty years. Here's a chance to have fun, be creative – oh, and to give a little thought to what your future is going to be! So get started on those costumes, and I look forward to seeing a glimpse into the future in a couple of weeks!"

That woke everyone up. An excited buzz broke out in the classroom.

"This is awesome, Sharpay!" Ryan cried, his

eyes sparkling. "Just think of all the possibilities! You could be a singer or an actress or a Broadway dancer–"

"Yes," Sharpay said softly, looking into the distance as if she could see her future unfolding before her. "I could be anything. But the one thing I will be is – a *star*!"

THE CRINGE FACTOR

Normally I'm a pretty cool cat. Not much rattles me, and I'm kind of known for being the class clown so thick skin is a requirement of the job. But everybody has an embarrassing moment (trust me - some people have a lot more!). My big shame came a while ago, but it scarred me for life. Maybe longer. My fourth grade teacher made me recite a love poem in front of everybody, in tights no less. Just when I thought it couldn't get any worse - bam! - the tights ripped and everybody laughed. I ran off the stage and never wanted to show my face again. So next time something really embarrassing happens to you, just remember, we've all been there. And at least you probably weren't wearing tights!

EMBARRASSING MOMENTS

Everyone has them, but your own always seem worse than anyone else's. The characters relive their most painful moments...

RYAN:

Normally, I'm the first one to be off book for any musical and play. That's one of my specialties, memorizing lines. It just comes naturally and I always kind of enjoyed seeing some of the other actors struggle with their lines. But a few years ago, during the Fall Play, I had the lead (of course!) and I also had the first line in the show. The curtain came up, the spotlight came on and I absolutely froze. Somebody had to feed the first line to me from offstage. Sharpay never let me hear the end of it!

GABRIELLA:

The first time I had to sing a solo in choir I almost died. Literally. I was so nervous I started hyperventilating just before it was time for me to sing. My dress felt too tight, my mouth was full of invisible cotton, my whole body was shaking. When it was time for the solo I fainted. I started to fall off the stage and would have landed right on my head, but luckily the boy next to me caught me!.

TAYLOR:

It will haunt me for all of my years. I got my report card at the end of eighth grade, fully expecting to see nothing but As across the board again, ensuring that I was class valedictorian. But THEN I saw a B+ for geography. A B+!! I'd never even gotten an A- before in any subject in my life. I was sure it was a mistake, but the teacher triple checked and it was correct. I was salutatorian. And absolutely mortified!!

SHARPAY'S GUIDE

Sharpay shares some of her top tips for keeping your cool and coping with embarrassment:

THE DECOY METHOD: When you've done something heinously embarrassing, see if you can distract attention away from yourself as fast as possible. I usually try to get everyone to look at Ryan, but anyone else will do really!

TO KEEPING YOUR COOL

THE TOO-COOL-FOR-SCHOOL METHOD: No matter how much your cheeks burn or how badly you want to bury your head in the sand, you can still rise above it and act like nothing at all happened. Thankfully, I have the supreme confidence to be able to pull this off. Hopefully you do, too.

THE MAKE-UP METHOD: If you don't distract and you just can't rise, keep blushes at bay with green cream. Keep some handy at all time for embarrassing emergencies! It's not the ideal solution, but then shame isn't exactly ideal either.

THE MANTRA METHOD: A mantra is something you repeat over and over. At least, I think so, but whatever. Just repeat this in your head: "I don't care. I am NOT embarrassed." Repeat it enough and you might just start believing it. But do not repeat it outside of your head, or people will think you're crazy for talking to yourself and that will just create more embarrassment!

SHADES OF RED

There's getting embarrassed and then there's REALLY getting embarrassed. See how some of your favourite Wildcats grade their embarrassments.

GRADE 1 - PUCE: **You turn up at a party and totally forget the name of the host who opens the door for you.**

GRADE 2 - RED: **You show up to a party not knowing that it's fancy dress and you're wearing jeans and a tee and everyone else is dressed as Dracula, Britney Spears, Batman...**

GRADE 3 - VOLCANIC LAVA: **You thought it was fancy dress and turn up as a chicken, but it's actually a posh black tie dinner.**

GRADE 1 – PUCE: **You are in the mall with your boyfriend and you are telling him a long story, only to turn and realize that he drifted off to a sports store five stores back.**

GRADE 2 – RED: **You are in the mall with your boyfriend and you get the laces on your shoes caught in the escalator. It jams and you have to wait for security to rescue you.**

GRADE 3 – VOLCANIC LAVA: **You are entering the mall with your boyfriend and you get your dress caught in the revolving door and it tears in two!**

GRADE 1 – PUCE: **You fall asleep in class and wake up to find yourself dribbling over your text book.**

GRADE 2 – RED: **You fall asleep in class but no one wakes you up because they're too busy listening to you blab in your sleep about the girl you really have a big secret crush on.**

GRADE 3 – VOLCANIC LAVA: **Having to recite poetry in front of an auditorium! Just super un-cool! I'd sooner eat live fire ants!**

RATE THE SHAME

Rate each of these embarrassing moments on a scale from 1 to 5, with 1 being mildly embarrassing and 5 being SO-EMBARRASSING-YOU-WANT-TO-CURL-UP-AND-DIE!

You were in charge of designing the set for the Winter Musical. On Opening night, one of the 'trees' you created falls over, knocking over another tree, knocking over another tree, knocking over another tree...

It's time for the big basketball game. The gymnasium is packed with friends and family waiting to watch you play. You discover, to your horror, that you forgot your uniform at home. It's too late to go and get it, so you have to use the only one still in the locker room, about five sizes too small.

You are in chemistry lab, performing an experiment that will determine a large part of your mid-term exam. You are confident that you know what you're doing, but perhaps too confident... As you pour one beaker of liquid into another, a huge mushroom cloud of blue smoke fills the room. The fire alarms go off, the school empties, and you realize you've probably failed the exam.

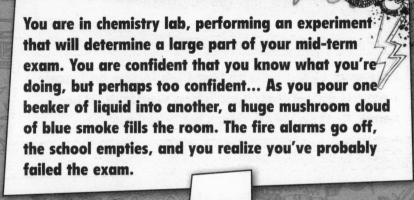

It's halftime and you and the other cheerleaders are performing a special routine you've been working on for weeks. All eyes are on you as you run out onto the court, when suddenly, uniform failure!! Your cheerleading skirt falls down around your ankles and you trip onto your face in front of everyone!

OLD WOUNDS

Some of your favourite East High faculty and staff share some of their humiliating memories. It just goes to show, some things never change!

COACH BOLTON: I was only a freshman basketball player but I thought I was pretty hot stuff. We were playing one of our big rivals and I really wanted to impress the varsity coach who was watching the game. I stole the ball at half court but got so spun around that I lost my sense of direction. I sped towards the basket as I heard everybody in the auditorium screaming. I fond out later they were screaming "STOP!" – I was heading towards the opponent's hoop and scored two points for the other team!

MS DARBUS: *It might be hard to believe, but I wasn't always the accomplished thespian that you see before you. In fact, when I was in high school I was notorious for forgetting lines. Well, I was determined to overcome my weakness, so I not only memorized my part in the Fall Play but everyone else's as well. I didn't miss a single one of my lines. However, the problem was that I repeatedly spoke half of the other actors' lines as well!*

MS BARRINGTON: I have always loved poetry, since my earliest days. Whenever I lacked the courage to say something to someone in person, I could always express myself in my poems. The problem was, my sister found my poetry notebook after we had a big fight. I had been harbouring a secret crush on a boy in school and had written countless poems about him. My sister made dozens of copies of the poems and taped them all around the school. I was so mortified I told the school nurse that I felt ill and went home.

ARE YOUR PARENTS EMBARRASSING?

You can choose a lot of things in life but unfortunately your family isn't one of them. Take this quiz to see just how embarrassing your parents really are.

1. AROUND CHRISTMAS YOUR MUM LIKES TO:

A. Tell goofy jokes about reindeer and snowmen

B. Sing Christmas carols for two weeks straight

C. Force you to go with her and sing carols for two weeks straight

D. Dress up like an elf while she puts up Christmas lights around the house

2. A BOY YOU REALLY LIKE DROPS BY THE HOUSE. YOUR DAD:

A. Asks him to sit down and watch sports with him

B. Asks 20 questions, each one more tough than the last

C. Says, "I'm sorry – there are no women of datable age living here. Come back in five years."

D. Threatens him with bodily harm

3. YOU MUM IS THE CHAPERONE AT THE SCHOOL DANCE. SHE:

A. Fusses over your dress a little too much, but otherwise stays out of the way

B. Hovers over you all night long, asking if you need anything

C. Tells your date there is to be no "huggy-kissy-face"

D. Repeatedly asks to dance with your date

4. YOUR DAD ATTENDS ONE OF YOUR SPORTING EVENTS. HE:

A. Cheers so loudly that he loses his voice for three days

B. Paints his face and body in school colours

C. Rushes out onto the field or court wearing his old school uniform

D. Berates the referee and throws a punch at another parent in the stands

5. YOUR MUM IS TEACHING YOU HOW TO DRIVE. SHE:

A. Lectures a little too long but finally lets you get behind the wheel
B. Questions every little move or decision you make
C. Squeals loudly in fear every time you approach another car
D. Refuses let you behind the wheel, and then drives off the road and into a ditch herself

6. YOUR DAD IS IN THE AUDIENCE AS YOU PERFORM IN A PLAY. HE:

A. Tries to give you flowers before the show (bad luck!)
B. Turns up in full costume to show his support
C. Laughs loudly and repeatedly even though the play is a tragedy
D. Approaches the director after the show and demands that you get more lines next time

7. YOU AND YOUR MUM BUMP INTO YOUR ENGLISH TEACHER AT THE GROCERY. SHE:

A. Excuses both of you quickly – she never liked English
B. Begins reciting poetry, badly
C. Begins lecturing the teacher on how to improve her syllabus
D. Demands that you receive more challenging assignments and homework

8. YOU ARE GOING SHOPPING WITH YOUR MUM. SHE:

A. Drags you to candle shops, antique shops, vitamin stores…
B. Wears something that might have been fashionable when she was in high school
C. Insists that you wear matching outfits
D. Tries to act like she's a teenager again!

9. IT'S YOUR BIRTHDAY. YOUR DAD:

A. Invites a small group and only
   makes one embarrassing speech
B. Shows a slide show of all your
   most awkward moments in life
   (leading up to this one!)
C. Has a little too much wine and
   sings, loudly and with enthusiasm,
   like he's the star of a musical
D. Jumps out of a birthday cake

ANSWER KEY:

IF YOU ANSWERED MOSTLY AS, YOUR PARENTS
ARE GENERALLY TOLERABLE AND DON'T
APPEAR TO GO OUT OF THEIR WAY TO SHAME
YOU PUBLICLY.
IF YOU ANSWERED MOSTLY BS, YOUR PARENTS
DON'T HUMILIATE YOU, BUT THEY CERTAINLY
DON'T DO YOU ANY FAVOURS WHEN YOU'RE IN
PUBLIC TOGETHER
IF YOU ANSWERED MOSTLY CS, YOUR PARENTS
HAVE A KNACK FOR EMBARRASSING YOU
ALMOST EVERY TIME YOU'RE TOGETHER.
IF YOU ANSWERED MOSTLY DS, YOUR
PARENTS ARE HOPELESSLY AND TRAGICALLY
EMBARRASSING. WE'RE REALLY, REALLY SORRY.

BLUSH BUDDIES

It's time to see which High School Musical character you share a sense of shame with. Look at the boxes below and tick off the things you might find really embarrassing. When you're done, check at the end to find out which character you would blush alongside-whoever you share the most ticks with.

1. Missing free throws ☐

   Singing for the first time in public ☐

   Admitting to your friends how much you like a boy/girl ☐

2. Wearing something that was popular last season ☐

   Singing off-key (although it almost never happens!) ☐

   Losing. At anything. ☐

3. Admitting a secret passion for something other people might not understand ☐

   Asking a boy / girl out and being rejected ☐

   Being yelled at by Coach ☐

4. Getting less than top marks on any test ☐

Admitting that you're wrong ☐

Showing your real emotions to a boy/girl ☐

5. Reciting poetry. Anywhere, but especially in public ☐

Being mistaken for a study nerd ☐

Messing up in sports ☐

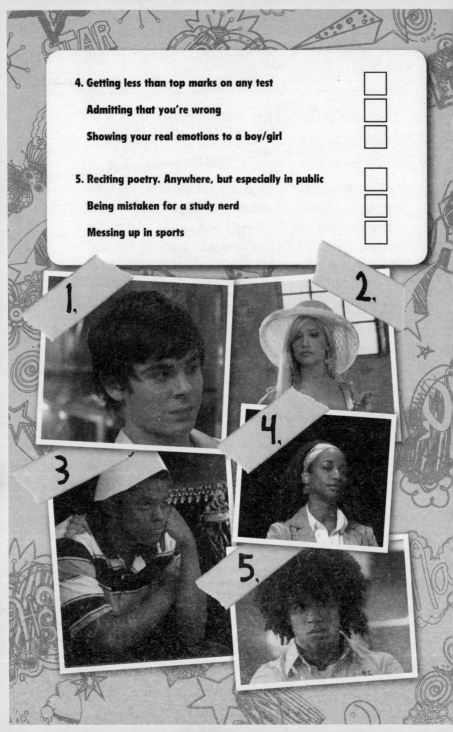